PANDORA'S
WAR

M.M. BAILEY

Pandora's War
Published in 2024 by
Matthew James Publishing
West Wing Studios
Unit 166, The Mall
Luton, LU1 2TL
matthewjamespublishing.com

Trigger Warning

This book contains scenes that may make some
readers uncomfortable, including those involving
violence, blood and descriptions of a sexual nature.

Action, violence and a delicious sprinkling of spice?
Welcome reader, you've come to the right place.
Don't worry it can be our little secret.

Acknowledgements

Taking the leap into the world of writing for adults has been one of the scariest and most exciting adventures I've embarked on. Jumping out of the box and exploring just how far I can push myself has been an experience I can't believe I waited so long for. But none of it would have been possible without so many other amazing people.

Without James and Ant at MJP for their belief in me, their support and for putting up with my million questions, *Pandora's War* would have never existed.

A huge thank you to Nicky and Teah for reading everything I've sent them at random times of the night.

I can't not thank Bob Stone enough for being my sounding board, my muse and often my voice of reason when I doubted myself over the last decade.

To author CJ Skuse who inspired me at Bath Spa Uni to push myself and allowed me the freedom to push my writing into the darkness I've so gladly begun to embrace (I don't think she realises the monster she unleashed, but it was like being given the keys and permission to write what I truly wanted for the first time).

And most importantly to my poor husband who supports me and pushes me always to chase my dreams, even when that means me writing at 3 a.m.

One

'I mean there's always the garage. It's already sheeted off and ready if you want him lifted?'

'No, no, no. That would require a clean-up crew afterwards and I can't be arsed with the mess. We'll try this a more subtle way.'

'You sure you're not going soft?' His deep chuckle was met with a steely glare.

'You want to test that theory?' An eyebrow arched accusingly.

'No,' he stuttered, loosening his collar. 'I mean I didn't mean any disrespect Boss.'

'Remember that.'

Her heels echoed as she exited the warehouse, wrapping the long blue trench coat around herself and tying the belt in a secure knot around her waist. Before she stepped out through the small metal door, an umbrella appeared, protecting her flame-red locks from the attack of rain.

Another figure waited, eyes squinted against the attack of wind, opening the car door as she approached and closing it promptly as she entered the blacked-out SUV.

'Where to, Boss?' the driver asked.

It was never Ma'am or Miss; just Boss. That told people all they needed to know.

'I'm not sure yet Wayne, I need time to think. Just drive please.'

'Yes, Boss.' He reached for the stereo, pressing play, the soothing tones of her favourites reaching out from the speakers, allowing her mind to drift.

This couldn't be rushed; she had worked too hard and had too much blood on her hands to lose everything now. Impulse always led to problems, she'd learnt that the hard way...

The hard assault of the rain on the roof was calming and entrancing as she lost herself in its rhythm, drowning out the song. She hated the cold chill of the rain but loved nothing more than listening to it in the darkness of the night, dreaming and planning.

A vibration in her pocket dragged her regretfully back to the moment.

'Yes? Okay, I'm on my way.'

Beep, beep beep...

'Wayne, take me to the club please.'

'Yes, Boss.'

The car turned swiftly, heading back in the direction they had just come. It turned right, then took the third left, pulling up softly outside a beautifully crafted entrance.

Limbo

'Hopefully, this won't take long, so don't go too far.'

'Yes, Boss.'

The black polished door opened and an umbrella was already erected, waiting for her. It still took some getting used to, but image was everything in this game. Her hips swayed hypnotically as she walked to the entrance and the two mountains parted, nodding as she glanced between them.

'Evening Boss,' they chanted.

'Evening boys.'

Lights twisted and sparkled as she took her usual route through the elegantly laid-out club. Her eyes glanced from figure to figure as they performed, each one beautifully sculpted, each one moving mesmerizingly to their captive audience and each one with a deadly secret. None stopped, none met her gaze, each focussed on their performance and immersed in the show they were giving.

As she approached the silver door to the left of the bar, a figure that dwarfed the two mountains at the front entrance looked down at her petite figure.

'Is she in there?'

'Yes, Boss.'

She nodded to him as he stepped aside, opening the door to the dark, descending corridor. Dim lights flicked on as she stalked through the darkness, not waiting for the lights to catch up. A dead end with a door greeted her. Impatiently she punched the code into the door and it beeped red.

'Stupid crap,' she mumbled to herself.

Second attempt, red again. Third attempt… green. The door clicked and she turned the handle, slipping inside and pulling the door quickly behind.

'Boss, sorry for calling so late, but I know you like to be here when…'

'Yes, you were right to call me, Frankie. Fill me in on the details.'

Frankie nodded, adjusting the stylish eye patch covering her left eye. Leading her over to the lounge seat, she stood over the quivering mess before her. She undid the jacket, leaving it on but open, crouching down with her bum resting on her black polished heels.

'It's okay, little one, you're safe now.' Her hands reached out to the matted bundle of dirty blonde hair and the figure it belonged to flinched, body shaking. She stroked the knotted mound, careful not to get her nails tangled.

Pushing her hands onto her knees she stood back up with a creak, wandering over to a large wooden desk. Taking the pressure off her feet, she sat on the swivelling chair behind it.

'She can't be more than fourteen, Frankie.'

'Dead on the money there, Boss,' Frankie nodded.

'Where did you find her?'

'They had her on the move…'

'And she was the only one?'

'No, but she was the only one still…'

'Okay, I get the point.' Her fist clenched, nails digging in as she resisted the urge to smash something in front of the child. 'Do we know her name?'

'Nora, Boss.'

'Do we know anything more?'

'No, Boss.'

'Take her to Felix. Keep me updated.'

'Yes, Boss.'

Lifting the small frame like a toy doll, Frankie headed through a wooden door adjacent to the one she had come in through, the child carefully in her arms. The door softly closed and she exploded,

3

rage pouring out as she cleared her desk across the room, a scream erupting.

A knock on the door, the biggest mountain's voice muffled.

'You okay in there, Boss?'

'Yes, Seb, I'm just redecorating.'

'Okay, Boss. Sorry for disturbing you. Let me know if you need any help.'

She smiled to herself, head in hands, and a small chuckle escaped. Reaching into her pocket she grabbed her phone. She cleared her throat and dialled.

'Hey, it's Pandora. We need to talk.'

Two

He checked his watch for the fourth time. They were late.

He wasn't a fucking dog to be summoned. No fucking respect. And no concept of time. This was what you got when you dealt with the devil. But he was fucking Miles Wyatt and nobody was stupid enough to cross him. Well almost nobody.

The crunching of pebbles, the blinding of the headlights and the hum of the engines drew his attention as the four dark cars pulled up. His hand twitched close to the cold metal inside his jacket; just in case.

A figure joined him on either side as the cars stopped.

'Keep a close eye, anything goes sideways you know what to do.'

They both nodded.

'Ah Mr Wyatt, thank you for joining me,' the drawling voice echoed from across the yard as a figure sloped out from one of the cars, approaching with open arms.

'Didn't really give me much choice, now did you, Joey? What the fuck is this all about?'

The tanned smile from Joey Siegel dropped with his arms and he raised a single index finger instead.

'You know exactly what this is about, my boy. If your father was still about, I doubt you'd be showing such disrespect,' Joey spat.

'Well he ain't about, is he? You're dealing with me and I want to know what the fuck was so important we're meeting in the scrap yard at 2 o'clock in the goddamn morning!'

'My fucking shipment, you little rat!'

His shipment. There were no shipments that this piece of scum had that would interest him. Joey was the lowest piece of crap going, dealing in everything from pimping to human trafficking.

These were lines that even Miles wouldn't cross. But Joey, there were no limits when money was involved.

'I have no idea what shipment you are on about and if you were stupid enough to bring anything in without putting it through my port that's your problem, Joey.'

Joey stood quietly. 'If I find out you had anything to do with this, boy, I'll destroy you.' His nostrils flared and his fists clenched. Miles bit back the urge to laugh; Joey was scum, but he was dangerous and had to be dealt with carefully. There was only one reason Joey wouldn't have run the shipment through the port; the cargo was live. Or at least it was when it was loaded.

'If that shipment was what I think it was, then you know it wouldn't have interested me. Which is why you didn't run it through the port with my protection. Believe me or not, I don't give a fuck. But as a gesture of goodwill, as you were so close with my father, I'll get the boys to put the feelers out,' Miles grinned.

'You better do boy. I want to know who has my shit and I want to know yesterday. And if I find out you have got anything to do with it, I'll cut off your balls and feed them to you raw!' Joey spat as he stormed back to his car, the wheels skidding as the cars reversed back out.

'Hmm…' Miles was intrigued.

His blond companion to the right spoke up first. 'What you thinking, Boss?'

'I'm thinking I'd like to find out who is screwing with Joey Siegel and buy the guy a drink,' Miles chuckled. 'Put out the word Jay, but nothing goes back to that dickhead, understand?'

Jay nodded, pulling out his phone and walking off dialling.

Miles headed back to his car, sliding into the back seat with a grin. There was a new player on the board, but were they going to be an ally or a threat? Shutting the car door, he tapped on the glass between him and the driver. 'Fuck it, I need a drink.'

The driver nodded, heading out of the scrap yard and back towards town. There was only one place Miles would drink at this time of night.

Temptation.

The queue was halfway down the road and the crowd was buzzing as Miles pulled himself out of the car. Walking past the crowds he got to the front of the queue.

'Hey man, back of the queue, you ain't a celeb you know,' barked a well-oiled guy who'd spent more time in the mirror than the two females hanging off him.

An eyebrow arched, he turned back to the testosterone-filled muscle-head. 'No, but it is my club.' The jaw drop was immediate.

'Ladies, would you like to come to VIP?'

The two well-manicured blondes immediately dropped their grip on the musclehead's arms and leapt out of the queue, escorted by Miles to the front where a dark-haired, toned man stood grinning at the unfolding situation. His arms were crossed against his well-pressed suit and tieless shirt.

'Two lovely ladies for VIP with a bottle of champagne on me please Mike.' Both girls squealed as Mike winked at them with his ice-blue eyes and led them off.

'No problem, Boss, I'll take good care of them,' he shouted. Miles patted the brutish-looking doorman on the shoulder, who nodded mutely before heading into the buzz of music and dancing. The lights flashed as several girls danced on podiums around the dancefloor. The bartenders flipped and twisted as the cocktails poured and the girls gathered, dreamy-eyed, waiting for their turn. Approaching the bar, Miles didn't even need to order as a bottle slid towards him. He picked it up, took a sip and the ice-cold beer slid down his throat.

'Thanks, Tom,' he shouted as the bartender nodded, carrying on with his aerial display for the ladies. Ascending the staircase, he climbed to the top level, entering VIP; the perfect vantage point to see all the fun. Nothing better than people-watching. Guys trying to flex their muscles rather than their brains. Girls trying to catch the eye of something tasty. Everyone on the hunt for something. Well almost everyone.

In the far corner of the club, two figures stood huddled, talking discreetly. One was Pixie, his best hostess. The other he didn't know. Flaming red hair, blue fitted trench coat and black heels. Not Pixie's type. The exchange lasted only minutes but his interest was piqued. Heading down the spiral staircase he managed to intercept the pair as they were about to part. The redhead crashed straight into his chest, stopping dead. As she looked up her eyes locked with his.

'I don't think we've had the pleasure,' Miles grinned. She raised an unimpressed eyebrow.

'Oh Mr Wyatt,' Pixie butted in, 'this is my friend, sir. She was just dropping off my keys as I left them at home.' Pixie jangled the keys hanging from her finger.

The redhead stayed silent, still holding his gaze. Few people did that. Not those that knew who he was anyway. He was intrigued.

'I'm Miles...' he gestured for her to reply.

'And I'm leaving,' she smirked, sidestepping him, but he stepped again to intervene. 'Nice to meet you 'Leaving', fancy a drink?'

'Maybe some other time, Mr Wyatt.'

'It's just Miles...'

'Well, Just Miles. Maybe some other time.' She sidestepped him again, patting his shoulder like a small pet before sauntering out of the club. He watched her hips sway towards the exit. It wasn't often he found himself speechless. He turned to quiz Pixie but she was already gone back to working the crowds and mingling with customers. Shaking the intrigue, Miles headed back up to the VIP. This wasn't the time for distractions. Not even ones as interesting as that.

Three

She hadn't planned on being seen. She hadn't planned on running into Miles Wyatt. She was just another face in a sea of many he would encounter. He would forget her by the morning. Hopefully.

Leaving the club, Pandora pondered her brief chat with Pixie. Joey Siegel was on the warpath. Joey Siegel was looking for the man who had fucked him over. Joey Siegel could go fuck himself. She chuckled to herself; he was looking in all the wrong places and his arrogance was just what she needed.

A car pulled up beside her as she strolled down the dimly lit street. The window rolled down slowly. A figure leaned out the window, his eyes feasting on Pandora's curves as his hand rubbed his tattooed neck.

'Hey, baby! Wanna ride?'

She didn't make eye contact or acknowledge the car's occupants, carrying on her stroll.

'Hey now, no need to be rude. Pretty gal like you shouldn't be walking home alone. Let us give you a lift.'

Pandora gritted her teeth and kept walking as the car crawled along matching her pace. She didn't have time for this.

'Hey!' The tone had a more demanding snap to it this time. 'I'm talking to you, bitch.'

Ah, there we go, she thought. There's the dickhead within surfacing. She stopped, hands both rooted in her trench coat pockets. He smirked, finally getting the attention he thought he wanted. Twisting her hips, she turned to face the car, her hips now swaying slowly as she approached the rolled-down window. Glancing in, she noted three figures; the cocky one in the front, another smirking in the back and a dainty little thing quivering next to him, clearly uncomfortable by the hand securely on her exposed thigh.

'Sorry boys, was in a world of my own. How rude of me.'

The men's grins widened as she bent over, one hand now on the car window frame. The neck tattoo on both was now clear enough to see who they belonged to: Joey Siegel.

'Don't worry, I'm sure you can make it up to us,' the backseat dickhead purred with a wink.

She knew she should just walk away; she knew what she should do. But she was never one to follow her own advice. Her hands trailed across the warm bonnet as she coaxed herself round the front of the car to the passenger door, eyes on her new friends. Opening the door, she slid into the front seat, exposing a flash of one leg as she sat. Twisting herself round to face the driver and take a glance at the rear passengers, she slowly bit her bottom lip, her left hand teasing from her knee up her thigh.

'Let's have some fun, boys.'

Before either could speak, her left hand had unclasped the gun from its strap.

Two shots. Front seat. Rear seat.

The one in the back slumped onto the poor girl with his hand still on her thigh. The quivering now escalating into a panic attack. Pandora sighed.

'Breathe girl, breathe.'

'Oh my God,' the girl gasped. 'What have you done?' The horror was etched into her gaping face.

'I believe I just shot them and saved you from a crappy night.' Pandora raised an eyebrow.

'You just signed my death. Mr Siegel is going to kill me,' she blubbered, a flood now cascading down her pretty face, mascara smudged across her cheeks.

'He'll have to go through me first.'

The blubbering ceased and the confusion set in. It didn't surprise her. They were taught this was a man's world. They were taught that they were under their control.

That's why they would never see her coming.

A short phone call later and three cars arrived. Pandora had managed to lure the quiverer from the back seat and even coaxed a name from her; Lila. Wayne appeared from the first car, a warm jacket in hand that he passed to Pandora. Turning to Lila, she wrapped it around her.

'Lila, you're going to go with Wayne here.' Lila's eyes widened, her previous interactions with men obviously playing in full HD in her mind.

'Hello Miss Lila,' said Wayne, his voice soft, keeping his distance. 'I'm here to escort you to somewhere safe.' His polite and professional approach seemed to be working as Lila's shoulders lost some tension. Pandora interrupted, 'Wayne, can you take her to Frankie for me? She's expecting her.'

'What about you, Boss?' he enquired.

'I'll make my own way back, Wayne.'

'Are you sure? You don't want another...'

'I said I'm fine Wayne,' she snapped, cutting him off. 'Just get her out of here before anyone sees her.'

Knowing when to back down he nodded, gently leading Lila to his car. She turned her head back before getting into the car.

'Thank you,'

Pandora nodded before addressing the other arrivals.

'Seb, make this look like a rival gang. I don't want any hint that links this to the shipments being hit.'

'Yes, Boss.'

Wiping her gun, she handed it to him. 'You'll probably need this,' she grumbled, it was one of her favourites. Not that you should have a favourite, but this one was reliable and easy to conceal. Needs must though.

'Nate, throw me the keys to your car. You can ride back with Seb once you're done.'

A set of keys was tossed towards her and she hopped into the empty car.

This was not how tonight was meant to go. First Miles Wyatt, then Joey Siegel's knob jockeys. But at least she had relieved him of some dead weight and managed to relocate Lila. Enough action for one night, time for some much-needed sleep. She yawned as she lowered the windows to keep her awake long enough to get home.

Her bed was calling and tomorrow was a new day.

Four

'Miles... Miles... MILES! Are you even listening to me, Boss?'

He was distracted and that was dangerous.

'Sorry Jay, I was thinking.' But thinking about the wrong thing.

'We are hitting dead ends,' Jay continued. 'It's like the shipment just vanished.'

'Do we know what was in it yet? Might give us an idea on who'd be stupid enough to hit it.'

Miles already had an idea, but Joey hadn't specified.

'Yes Boss, it was a shipment of girls,' his voice trailed off confirming. Ask Jay to kneecap someone, no problem, ask him to pimp out a girl, he'd rather cut his own balls off. One of the many reasons Jay worked for Miles and not Joey.

Running his hands through his soft dark hair, Miles sighed. 'Should have known, but I'm not sure who would be twisted enough or stupid enough to pull this off.'

'We've dug into all the local players and none of them seem to be involved, or if they are, they are hiding it pretty well. There's one thing that I don't get though, Boss...'

'And that is?'

'What's happening to the girls? They haven't appeared in any of the other venues, there's been no auctions. It's literally like they've vanished off the face of the Earth,' Jay replied, scratching the back of his neck.

'That's a good point, but Joey still thinks I'm involved so we need to find at least something to get him off our backs. There must be some way to trace the transport. Speak to Joey's boys and find out what they were being transported in and see what you can do from there.'

A gentle knock came on the door. Pixie popped her head in.

'Mr Wyatt, you asked to see me?' She clung to the door, not entering further than necessary.

Miles's ears perked up. 'Ah yes, Pixie come in. Jay, would you excuse us please?'

Jay raised an eyebrow before sloping off, throwing a curious glance between the two.

'Pixie, have a seat,' Miles gestured to the chair.

Lowering herself slowly into the chair, Pixie glanced around looking anywhere but at her boss.

'Did I do something wrong, Mr Miles?' she squeaked.

'No, Pixie, not at all, you're my best hostess. I just wanted to ask you a question.'

A gulp escaped Pixie, her hands rubbing together and her foot tapping slightly.

'Yes sir?'

'Your friend, from the other night; I've never seen her before.'

'She was just dropping off my keys, sir. I'm sorry, I know we're not meant to have people visit us at work, I promise it won't happen again.' Her eyes dropped to the floor, glued to the carpet at her feet.

'No, it's fine. I'm just curious. What's her name?'

'Her name?'

'Yes... name. People usually have them.'

'Erm it's,' she hesitated, 'it's Pandora, sir.'

'Pandora.' He liked the way it rolled off his tongue. 'And does she work in one of the clubs?' Most girls with half-decent looks made their money in the clubs, well, all those except the ones that belonged to Joey.

'Oh God no sir,' she blurted out, her hand flying to cover her mouth.

'Well, where does she work then?'

He could see her trying to work out if she should tell him, she thought she had a choice in the matter. He leaned in and placed a hand on either arm of the chair, giving her no option but to look at him.

'What's the matter Pixie, why won't you tell me where she works? Does she have something to hide? Do you have something to hide?'

13

'No, no sir,' she reassured. 'She, erm, she works in a bookshop and she's just a very private person. She'd be very upset with me if she knew I was talking about her to you.'

'Don't worry, it will be our little secret,' he winked. 'I was just being nosey. You can go now Pixie, I'm sure you've got plenty to do.'

'Yes sir, plenty.'

He moved his arms, standing tall and allowing Pixie to make her escape.

Pandora. The distraction he hadn't wanted. He thought he'd be satisfied once he knew her name. He wasn't.

He had forgotten to ask which bookshop she worked at. No point calling Pixie back, he'd already stressed her enough it would seem. His thoughts rolled back to Pandora. A girl that intriguing shouldn't be cooped up in a bookshop. Picking up the handset from the phone on his desk, he dialled a number. 'Hey Ryan, can you get me a list of bookshops in town? Yes, I said bookshops. Thank you.' The phone clicked as he ended the call.

There was a vibration in his pocket. He reached in and grabbed his phone.

'Yes... When?... Last night? For fuck's sake!'

The tone went dead. This wasn't good. Two of Joey Siegel's top guys had been shot by a rival gang and one of Joey's favourite toys, Lila, was missing.

This was going to mean war.

But with whom? Someone had a fucking death wish and it wasn't going to be swift once Joey got a hold of them.

Five

'You told him what?' Pandora growled.

'I'm sorry, Boss, I panicked!'

'A bookshop! A fucking bookshop, Pixie? Do I look like a pissing librarian?' Pandora shook her head in disbelief. 'And you told him my name!' Her day was just going to shit, minute by minute.

'I didn't mean to, Boss, I was trying to think quickly but he was pushing for answers and I blurted it out.'

Pandora let out a frustrated groan.

'But why a bookshop, Pixie? Of all the places?'

'He had a bookcase behind his desk and it was the first thing I saw.' She hung her head.

'For fuck's sake! Now I'm going to have to buy a bookshop!'

'Really?' Pixie questioned.

'Yes, really. I can't have anyone knowing what I do. Not when we've got so much at stake.'

'I am sorry, honestly. I just wasn't expecting him to even remember you.'

'That makes two of us. At least you didn't tell him who I really am.'

'But I told him your name, Boss.'

'It won't matter. By the time we're done, everyone will know it eventually. Right, you better head back, don't want you being late. Report back to me later with anything of use.'

Pixie nodded, grabbing her bag and heading out, throwing an apologetic look back at Pandora.

Frankie, who had been sat silently through the exchange, smirked.

'And what may I ask do you find so funny?'

'Well, at least she didn't tell him you were a singer, because there's no way on Earth we could fake that.' Frankie let out a chuckle, amusing herself.

'Fuck you, dickhead,' Pandora replied with a middle finger extended. It was true though, she thought, slightly amused. Some things were beyond even her skills.

***

Pandora sat, thinking.

Miles Wyatt. That overconfident swagger. The power that he controlled with a mere glance.

She knew she'd made a mistake the minute she'd made eye contact, but she wasn't one for backing down and that had been her screw-up. He wasn't part of the plan. He wasn't on her list; at least not yet. He had a code of sorts, or at least that's what Pixie had reported back. No children, no pimping, no trafficking. His girls were well-paid and well-treated. He didn't mix business and pleasure. But he was still dangerous, so he needed watching. Pixie was the best when it came to recon. So dainty and soft, nobody would ever notice her, but she saw and remembered everything.

Pandora had known she'd be perfect to place at Temptation. Pixie was a bit nervous at first but had soon settled in and was making herself good money while she was at it.

A knock came at the door, this time it was Seb. The giant gently opened the door.

'Hey, Boss, you said you wanted an update?'

Pandora nodded for him to continue.

'We set it up like you asked and they took the bait. They are now on the warpath but have no clue which gang did it. Everyone is on tenterhooks.'

A war was brewing. Not ideal, but it took the attention away and gave her a much-needed distraction.

'One other thing, Boss...'

'Yes?'

'Miles Wyatt has had his boys digging about the missing shipments.'

Seb headed back out, the door handle clicking as he closed it. Miles Wyatt. How many times in a day would that name pop up?

He was getting closer to being added to the list, thought Pandora. But why was he sniffing around Joey's business? If Pixie was right, Miles had nothing to do with that type of business, so why shove his nose in? He was becoming more of a pain in the ass by the minute, but she didn't need him sticking his nose in her business.

Too many unexpected variables. Too many distractions. This couldn't affect the plan. She'd worked too hard and lost too much to let any of this get in the way. The next few moves were vital and she couldn't afford any more hiccups.

She thought back to Lila, there were no regrets there though. She'd do it all again in a heartbeat and that was before she knew Lila was one of Joey's toys. Even the thought left her fists clenched and teeth gritted, resisting the urge to smash something. Pandora knew exactly what kind of treatment Lila would have gone through without even seeing the scars or the fear in the poor girl's eyes. A fate no woman should have to endure.

Pandora's attention was drawn to the corner of the room. Frankie was sat tapping away on her phone, grinning.

'What are you doing?' Pandora demanded, being pulled from her reflections.

'Finding you a bookshop to buy of course,' Frankie replied, winking with her one eye.

There weren't many people with the balls to cheek Pandora, but Frankie had been there from the start. If it wasn't for Pandora, she would have been missing more than just an eye. But she had seen the Boss before she became the Boss and seen the transformation as the mouse turned into the lion.

God help anyone who became her prey.

Six

Over a week of searching. Three left.

Who knew there were so many bookshops in town? Who knew so many people actually read? Miles was a fan of reading, but it didn't really fit with his image, so the chance to sneak off and grab a few chapters of something was few a far between. Most of the bookshops were owned by older people or couples and none had heard of a Pandora. But Pixie wouldn't have lied, she couldn't lie to save her life, Miles had discovered that the first week she worked there.

One of the girls, Maxine, had been roughed up by a customer and was scared of Miles finding out. Pixie had tried to hide it, but Miles had gotten the truth out of her. Maxine had been given the rest of the week off with pay to recover and Pixie had been promoted to hostess so she could be his eyes and ears on the floor. The jackass who got too handsy ended up with thirty-seven breaks and a warning not to return.

Looking for bookshops was not going to do his image or reputation any good if anyone spotted him, but he was Miles Wyatt, he did what he wanted, when he wanted. Fuck everyone else. Well almost.

His phone rang right on cue, he looked at the caller ID
Joey Siegel
'Yes?'
'Do you have an update?'
'Not yet...'
'Well, you better get one soon boy, or I might start thinking you had something to do with all this...'
The line when dead. The guy was a cunt. But he was a dangerous

one and Miles couldn't deny the fact. He was also an impatient one. Miles was going to start running out of time.

Jay had already voiced his concerns about unnecessary distractions, yet here he was outside yet another shop.

Books and Banter

As he entered through the battered old blue door a bell rang, catching the attention of a frail figure.

'Just one moment and I'll be with you,' the voice croaked. The old man placed down the books he had been carrying and headed slowly over to Miles.

'What can I do for you, good sir?'

He obviously doesn't know who I am, thought Miles, and putting on his politest voice he replied, 'I'm looking for a girl.'

'Wrong place for that my boy, most people do that at the dances,' the old man chuckled.

'No,' interrupted Miles, 'I'm looking for a specific girl, one that works at a bookshop. Her name is Pandora.'

The old man faltered. He knew the name. He paused for a second, contemplating.

'Pan, my dear… there's someone here for you,' he hollered.

Miles could hear footsteps from behind the scenes. A few moments later the sight of red curls appeared.

'Yes, Boss?' she quipped affectionately.

'This young man is looking for a girl called Pandora. I think he means you.' He winked at her, toddling off back to his books.

The smile dropped from Pandora's face. 'Mr Wyatt, fancy seeing you here. Have you come to buy a book?'

'Yes, actually and I was told you were the perfect person to come to for a recommendation,' Miles smirked. She was at work and as long as he was a customer, she would have to interact with him.

'What type of book were you looking for, Mr Wyatt?' she emphasised his name for formality.

'I'm… open to suggestions,' he grinned playfully.

She intrigued him.

Her eyes were still locked with his chilly blue ones, something he was unfamiliar with. Most men couldn't look him in the eyes let alone this tiny dot of a woman. But something told him there was fire in her eyes and he was itching to feel that heat.

'How about Beauty and The Beast?' she snarked.

'Tempting, always something tempting about a classic but I like a book with a bit more spark, something more… feisty.'

His phone buzzed from his pocket but he ignored it, waiting for her response. Everything about her was hostile but somehow made him want to provoke her more.

'Aren't you going to answer that, Mr Wyatt? It could be your girlfriend, or your mother, worried about where you are.' Her lips edged a daring smile.

'I don't have a girlfriend and my mother only calls on Sundays,' he retorted with a smirk.

The phone continued to buzz; he took it out.

Joey Siegel

He headed outside to answer it, putting some space between him and Pandora.

'Yes…'

'Tick tock, boy…'

'Well, the more you ring me, the more of my time you are taking away from finding them.'

'Don't forget who you are talking to boy.'

The line went dead and Miles grunted to himself. Couldn't he get off his fat arse and find the fuckers himself? Of course not, that would mean engaging his brain and possibly getting his hands dirty and that just would not do.

Heading back inside, he scanned the shop looking for the flash of red hair.

'If you're looking for Pandora, my boy, she's finished for the day,' said the old man, rearranging the books on the shelf in front of him.

A frustrated pang of annoyance hit Miles. Damn, Joey. Oh well, he knew where she worked now.

He didn't know why she was so distracting but he was determined to work it out and get her out of his system. Then he could get back to focussing on what really mattered.

Work.

Seven

'He's gone my dear, you can come out…'

Waiting a few more seconds, Pandora scanned the shop from the storeroom. Once she was sure, she stepped out.

'Friend of yours my dear?'

'I wouldn't exactly use the word friend in the same sentence as him, Boss,' she said with an affectionate curl of her lips.

'That should be me calling you Boss, my dear. After all, you did buy the place.'

Pandora turned to the frail man grinning at her. 'I may own it on paper, but it will always be yours and in these four walls you will always be Boss.'

'I get the feeling that owning a bookshop wasn't part of your plan, my dear?'

He got that right, thought Pandora. 'No, it wasn't. But they do say some of the best decisions are those that are unexpected.'

She watched as he slowly worked his way around the counter, he never stopped. Frankie had done some background on him. Mr George Talbot, 78 years old, had been the owner for over fifty years. No family, his wife and daughter were deceased, the bookshop was his life. She wasn't going to take that away from him, but she did have an idea.

Taking out her phone she quickly typed a message, the whoosh as it sent vibrating in her hands. She grabbed a pile of books and began to help sorting them.

'You don't need to do that, my dear, he's gone now.' He seemed confused. The agreement had been drawn up that Pandora would buy the business but George would still get to run it. She didn't need to pretend; the young gentleman was gone.

'Happy to help George, I've got a bit of time on my hands, I'm waiting for someone.'

Half an hour later, the pair sat and Pandora brought them both a cup of tea. It was just the two of them; George didn't deserve to see the other side of her. He knew vaguely what she was but he wasn't a threat. They sat comfortably enjoying each other's presence as Pandora read aloud from a book she'd taken to.

'Words have no power to impress the mind without the exquisite horror of their reality,' she muttered to herself.

'Edgar Allen Poe, I believe my dear.'

Pandora nodded. The old boy knew his stuff. The bell rang, signalling someone in the shop.

'We are busy today, never normally see so many people in one afternoon,' George said, delighted.

Taking a final sip, Pandora rose looking at the two newcomers.

'George, these aren't customers. These are… some close friends of mine.'

'Delighted! So nice to be surrounded by so many pleasant young ladies. I'm getting spoilt in my old age. Oh, I recognise you, you're the lovely lady who came to me about buying the shop.'

Frankie grinned, nodding at George. 'Hi Mr Talbot, this is my friend Nora.'

Pandora looked curiously at Nora, no longer the tangled mess they had retrieved that night, her long silky blonde hair had been unmatted and her pale skin now looked rosier and fresher. She smiled shyly at Mr Talbot.

Even with everything Nora had been through, she was still a delicate child. Her eyes wide and still full of hope made her too fragile for the life they led. Frankie was reluctant to let her stay in their world any longer than necessary, especially at her age.

Pandora had found the solution.

'George, this young lady here is Nora, she is in need of a job and a trade.' George's eyes widened as Pandora continued. 'Nora isn't quite old enough or suited, should we say, to my other lines of business, so I was wondering if you could be so kind as to do me one more favour.'

'Always room for a bright young apprentice here my dear,' George interrupted, seeing where the conversation was going.

His wife and daughter may have passed many years ago, but that fatherly look was still glowing brightly.

Nora approached nervously. 'Hi, Mr Talbot.'

'George, my dear, call me George.'

'I'd be happy to help and learn and I won't be any trouble, I promise, George,' Nora whispered, her previous experience with most adults still shaking her.

'Where's the fun without a bit of trouble?' He grinned. 'You can have my daughter's room. It will be nice to have some company around the place my dear. I hope you like hot chocolate?'

Nora nodded.

Pandora looked between the pair, happy with the arrangement.

'Nora, if you are happy to, then you will stay here with George and help him run the shop. You need to report back to me on anything suspicious and if you see this man...' She showed her a picture of Miles Wyatt. 'Remember, I am Pandora, who works here with you both. Nothing more, nothing less.' Nora nodded. 'And if you don't think you can lie, act shy and don't talk, Mr Talbot will do the rest.'

Nora blushed; the shy bit came naturally to her.

Frankie, who had been browsing the books, jerked her head back realising this was her bit. Taking a black rucksack off her back she placed it on the counter.

'Right Nora my dear,' reaching into the bag she started pulling bits out. 'Here we go, birth certificate, passport, a phone with our numbers programmed in, a laptop to keep you entertained, some cash if you need anything and a bank card. No holidays to exotic places, but if you need clothes or anything essential don't hesitate to pop it on there.' Frankie finished with her trademark one eye winking.

Nora took the card uneasily, looking at Pandora.

'Go on, take it, child. I'm trusting you.'

The look wasn't of fear, but something else, something much deeper and more powerful.

Respect.

'Right George, I've got a few matters to attend to, I'll leave you and Nora to get acquainted and I'll be back for my next shift in a few days if anyone asks.'

He nodded as Pandora took her leave, followed by Frankie who had just finished squeezing Nora.

As they left the shop, they headed to Frankie's dark blue car. Pandora hopped in the front passenger seat as Frankie roared the engine to life.

'You think we made the right choice, Boss?'

'Yeah, I think we made the only choice. The child fainted at the sight of a nosebleed, so she'd get herself or someone else killed if we tried to train her. She's too young and innocent. Maybe one day that will change but for now, she's in the perfect place.'

Pandora had many acquaintances, some like Seb and Wayne were built hard and strong, while others like Pixie and Nora were a little more delicate, but each had a role and they were her responsibility.

She protected her own.

Eight

The rotting stench was overpowering, even from a distance. Miles tried not to gag, but he could practically taste the decay of death in his throat. Using his sleeve, he covered the lower part of his face in a vain attempt to compose himself. He approached his men who were all busy scurrying about.

'Boss, this is definitely it,' Jay confirmed, lifting his mask and gloves off as he approached.

The missing shipment.

The truck had been stashed badly. They wanted it to be found. But why?

'I'm assuming there was no…?'

'No Boss. None. By the look of it, none of the bodies in the truck reached land alive.'

'That doesn't mean that there weren't any survivors though. They could have taken anyone who was left and just dumped the truck, but why not burn it and get rid of the evidence? It doesn't make any sense.'

Jay shook his head. 'No idea Boss, the whole thing is fucked up. But when is anything involving Joey not screwed in the head? He's a fucking sicko that one!'

Miles didn't disagree. Grabbing his phone, he dialled reluctantly.

'Yes, boy?'

Miles cleared his throat, 'I've found your missing truck.'

'And the contents?'

'Expired.'

Miles pulled the phone away from his ear as the rage and incoherent screams flooded his head.

'Do you want me to bring you the truck?'

'Are you stupid, boy? Burn it and its contents.' There was a brief pause. 'Did you hear me boy?'

'Yes, I heard you loud and clear.'

The line went dead.

'What did he say, Boss?'

'Burn it all...' Miles trailed off.

'Is that what you want me to do, Boss?'

Miles paused for a second, Joey's words lingering, no remorse, no empathy. A true sociopath through and through.

'We don't have a choice at this point.' His stomach twisted. Cremation or burial, it made no difference, there was no bringing them back. They died like caged animals, but they avoided a far worse fate in the end.

With a sigh, Miles glanced back to the truck once more before returning to the car. He was no closer to finding out who stole the shipment, but he did wonder if anyone had survived. Not that he was going to put that idea into Joey's head. No woman or child deserved the fate Joey Siegel had in store for them. But as much as Miles hated it, there was nothing he could do. Business was business. But it would never be his business.

He needed to clear his head. This was getting messy. Fast.

'Take me to Blend.'

'Yes, Boss,' replied the driver.

***

Blend was one of the most exclusive clubs Miles owned. In his words, it was the right blend of everything needed for a perfect night out. But its location was perfect for several other reasons too. Especially when Miles needed privacy.

Pulling up to the entrance, Miles was greeted by a smile. The door was opened by a grey-haired gentleman with rounded glasses.

'Evening sir, I wasn't expecting you until later.'

'Plans changed Bob, is everything ready?'

'As requested, sir, ready as always.'

Miles nodded, heading into the club and straight to the office on the ground floor. He shut the door behind him, opening another entrance behind the bookcase on the far wall. A steep metal staircase let him down to the basement level, deep below

Blend, soundproof, escape proof and nice and quiet for working in. It wouldn't stay quiet for long though.

His footsteps echoed off each step as he descended. The light flickered in the dimly lit room ahead, the outline of a figure sat slumped on a singular chair. Hair fallen in front of the figure's face, a puddle around the legs of the chair. Ropes neatly holding him secure.

'He's already pissed himself twice, Boss, and passed out and that was before I asked anything!' The large frame said stepping into the light. 'I ain't even touched him yet, just like you said!'

'Don't worry Lenny, you're fine. Just pass me that bottle of water.'

Miles took the bottle from the dark-haired brute's hand. Twisting off the bottle cap he took a small sip, eyes still firmly on the figure. Approaching, he ran his hands through the figure's hair firmly grasping a chunk, pulling the man's head back and pouring the water onto his face, before stepping back to wait.

Surprise and spluttering brought the man back around, his eyes widening as he saw the source of the water.

'Now Romano, let's have a little chat, shall we?'

A muted nod responded.

'Let's start with what you know about Joey Siegel's shipment.'

'I don't know anything Mr Wyatt, honest, I know nothing.'

'Okay, what about the hit on Joey's boys?'

'I don't know anything about that either sir, I promise I don't.'

Miles sighed, scratching his head.

'Okay Romano, let's try one last question. What do you know about Joey's business?'

Romano stuttered, 'Joey was bringing in girls. Everyone knows that. He wasn't exactly quiet about it. Some he kept for himself, others he sold off, well, those that survived the journey,' he chuckled nervously.

The chuckle.

Miles's fists clenched. He needed answers. Self-control was required.

'Good boy, Romano. Next question. Who was interested in taking Joey's business?'

Romano spluttered, 'Are you mad? Nobody would be stupid enough to try. Joey is untouchable, even you know that.'

Nobody was untouchable, thought Miles. But everything had a cost.

'Can I go now? I've told you everything I know.'

'One last question Romano… Were you buying girls off Joey?'

'Of course I was, I wasn't turning down profit like that,' Romano chuckled again, his shoulders now relaxing. 'You know what I mean don't you, can't tell me you've never…'

Miles stayed silent. He eyed the stainless-steel table to the left of Romano. Lazily he wandered over, his fingers trailing across the selection of tools laid out.

'So, can I go now?' Romano asked, 'I've got places to be, people to see you know.'

'I'd like to hear a bit more about how you're making this profit Romano, you've got me intrigued… I've got to admit, it's not a business I've ever… entertained.'

Romano paused, staring at Miles's back.

'Well, erm. It's all about making sure they know their place as soon as you get them. You know what I mean?'

Miles nodded. 'Continue…'

'The younger the better really. Easier to make them believe you'll go hurt Mommy and Daddy if they don't comply.' His tongue started to loosen, his grin expanding as his ego was stroked.

Miles picked up a flaky nail, rolling it between his fingers and watching the rust as he continued listening.

'Then it's all about breaking them in, I prefer doing that myself, gotta have some enjoyment if you know what I mean. Especially with the fresh ones.'

Miles picked up the hammer, turning back towards Romano, whose grin sank off his face.

'Go on…' Miles gestured him to continue, nail in one hand, hammer in the other.

'Well, I'm not quite sure what else there is to tell you. I know you're a busy man, so if you want to untie me I can be on my way, no bother to you.' Romano's voice cracked as a bead of sweat rolled slowly down the side of his face.

Miles stepped closer, silently.

Before he could reach Romano, another pool of piss began to seep down Romano's light beige trousers and onto the floor. He brought himself down to eye line with Romano, who was now quivering once again, snot sludging down over his lip.

'Please,' he begged. 'Please I'll do anything,'

'Anything?'

'YES!'

'Did they beg you like you're begging me, Romano?'

Romano's eyes widened.

'Did they cry and plead like you are, Romano?'

The silent fear engulfed the bound figure as the realisation hit him. Romano watched as Miles gently placed the nail on his crotch, swiftly followed by the brutal slamming of the hammer smashing the nail right through his ball sack, impaling him to the chair.

The screams subsided, followed by the whimpering escaping Romano's lips. A new stain appeared on his trousers, darker and thicker than the piss. The blood seeped out, as he tried not to move.

'Now you have a choice, my friend. I'm going to untie you. You can either stand up and let the nail rip through your right nut or let me shoot you in the head. Your choice.'

Miles stood back, dropping the hammer to the floor as he admired his work. A smile crept across his face.

Gasping, Romano's eyes darted around the room, pain blocking his ability to think. Lenny untied the ropes, letting Romano slump forward slightly, the pain hitting him in waves every time he moved, even slightly.

'Tick tock, Romano, I haven't got all day…'

Teeth gritted, Romano braced himself, hands on the armrest and ready to push up…

'I can't do it, I just can't,' he screamed. 'Please, just make it stop.'

Placing a hand under his jacket, Miles stepped forward.

'Now that I can do.'

He raised the gun.

The shot echoed around the basement. Romano slumped, the hole in his forehead leaking blood that slowly seeped down his blank face.

'Lenny, can you take it from here?'

'Yes, Boss.'

Miles turned, ascending the staircase with a smile on his lips. That was definitely the stress relief he needed to finish the day.

Nine

The tears flowed freely down Lila's face.

'Not long now, you're nearly done,' the gruff voice reassured her.

The buzzing continued as her hands gripped her kneecaps tighter. She nodded, trying not to move. Pandora watched silently from across the room. The tears continued, but Lila never made a sound. The steely look as her gaze stayed locked with Pandora's eyes told her all she needed to know. Lila was a fighter. She'd survived Joey for all these years and her fire was still in there. It had just needed a spark.

'All done.'

'Thanks Duke,' Lila whispered, standing with a strained stretch.

'Wanna see?'

Her eyes lit up and she nodded.

Grabbing a mirror, he stood behind her, his large, tattooed frame holding the small mirror up with a goofy grin as she looked at her reflection. Where once she had dreaded looking at the branded crown Joey had gifted her, now she saw a beautiful and intricate Celtic knot.

Her chains had been broken. She was now free.

Bouncing giddily on the spot, she turned to Pandora for approval. Pandora raised an eyebrow.

'You don't need my approval. It's your body and nobody owns it but you...' Pandora paused. 'But yes, Duke has done a stellar job as always.'

'Thanks, Boss,' the gruff voice replied. He blushed as he removed his gloves.

'Do we really have to do the hair, Boss?' whined Lila.

'Yes.'

'But it took me so long to grow it, couldn't I just dye it?' Lila pleaded, trying her best puppy dog eyes.

'No.'

'But—'

'The answer is no Lila. The hair goes, and so does the colour. No arguments.' Pandora shut her down. There was no room for debate.

'Duke, make her unrecognisable,' Pandora demanded.

'Yes, Boss,' Duke replied, scissors and hair dye in hand.

'What?' Lila gasped. 'Duke can't cut my hair.'

'He can and he will.' Pandora got up exasperated. She didn't have the energy for debate. Lila was becoming as bad as Frankie. At least when people were scared of her they didn't argue back. She didn't see the problem; Duke always did her hair and it never looked better. Stepping out of the room to drown out Lila's moaning, Pandora grabbed her phone from her pocket. Message from Frankie.

Bookshop.

Popping her head back in, Pandora interrupted the two who were currently arguing over hair colour.

'Duke, something's come up. Ring Wayne when you're done and he'll come and grab Lila.' Duke nodded. 'Lila, don't be a pain for Duke, it took me years to find someone as talented as him.' Lila nodded, eyes down. 'Duke, go for the brunette on her. It will throw anyone looking for a blonde.' Duke nodded again; thankful the choice had been made.

Pacing out of the back door, she headed down the alleyway. The bookshop was only a few roads over and walking would be quicker with the traffic and attract less attention. Cutting down the side road that led to the back of the shop she stopped for a second, catching her breath before slipping in the back door. She could already hear the voices chatting away.

That cocky tone she'd recognise anywhere.

'I'm lucky to have her, Mr Wyatt,' George's light tones quipped. 'Ah and speak of the devil, I think that's her back off her lunch break now. Pan is that you my dear?'

Gritting her teeth Pandora took a breath. 'Yes Mr Talbot, I'm back, sorry I'm a few minutes late.'

'Nonsense my dear you are right on time. You have a visitor.' George grinned as Pandora entered the shop floor.

'Pandora.'

'Mr Wyatt.'

Pandora bit her lip, reminding herself to tone it down. Her defiance was what had got her in this position in the first place.

'To what do we owe the pleasure, Mr Wyatt?' His name rolled off her tongue like silk.

'Well, we didn't finish our chat last time… you were helping me find something.' He stared at her lips, watching her bite her lower one slowly.

'Ah yes, how could I forget? I have the perfect one just for you.'

She slowly reached her hand under the counter, brushing past the concealed gun and, grabbing a dusty old book she'd been looking at earlier, she placed it on the counter with a thud.

Moby Dick.

'A tale of chasing the elusive,' she raised an eyebrow.

'Sounds like my kind of book. Does he catch it in the end?' Miles asked, the smirk still firmly planted.

'Well, that would spoil the surprise. Can't be ruining the ending now can I?' Pandora said, folding her arms.

His phone rang. She saw the irritated glare he gave the screen.

'Don't let me interrupt, Mr Wyatt,' said Pandora as she gestured to the phone.

'It's Miles remember, just Miles,' he said his smile returning as he placed the phone on the counter, grabbing his wallet out to pay for the book.

'I get the feeling that not everyone calls you just Miles,' Pandora said accusingly, as she delicately wrapped the book.

'You're right.'

The phone rang again, this time she managed to quickly glance at the caller ID as she leaned over to pass him the book.

Joey Siegel

What was he doing with that piece of shit? He continued to ignore the phone. 'How about a drink? You can give me a few more book recommendations.'

His proposal caught her off-guard. She quickly composed herself before replying, 'I don't drink.'

The phone continued to buzz, she could see his teeth clench as he tried to ignore it.

'You sure you don't need to get that? Seems important,' Pandora suggested, hoping to hear a glimpse of the conversation. She wanted to know how Miles Wyatt was connected to Joey. Information was worth more than all the weapons and money in the world.

'It's nobody important my dear. So, you don't drink, how about lunch? You do get a lunch break, and you must eat at some point, so why not?' he said trying to back her into a corner. She didn't like where this was going. She needed to be a faceless figure. She couldn't have anyone knowing. But... could Miles get her closer to Joey?

'Okay, tomorrow, but I only have half an hour so don't be late.' She left him speechless as she turned to walk away.

'See you tomorrow, Just Miles.'

Ten

'Boss, are you even listening?' Jay snapped.

'Yes of course I am,' he replied, still staring into space.

'What did I say then?' Jay crossed his arms with an annoyed smirk.

'That I'm the best Boss in the world for not cutting your tongue out for being a disrespectful little shit.'

'No, actually that's not what I said.'

'But you were thinking it.'

'Yes… of course, Boss.' Jay rolled his eyes.

'Go on then, what did you actually say?' Miles sighed.

'That you have a meeting today at lunch.'

'No.'

'No?'

'You heard me,' Miles growled, 'I said no, rearrange. I have plans.'

'One, you never have plans unless it's after 7 p.m. and with a hot blonde. Two, this is a massive meeting, you've been waiting for this deal for six months. Three, who the fuck are you and what have you done with Miles Wyatt?' Jay quizzed with a frown.

Closing in on Jay across the office, Miles grabbed him by the throat, slamming him into the wall, squeezing just hard enough to stop him talking.

'Jay, listen closely because I'm only going to say this once.' Jay's eyes widened. 'Rearrange the meeting, don't question my motives and remember who the fuck you are talking to. If you can't control your tongue, I'll relieve you of it. Understand?' Jay nodded.

Releasing his grip, Miles watched as Jay rubbed the red band decorating his neck. Miles tolerated Jay; he'd been with him a long time. But he was overstepping his boundaries and that wasn't going to be tolerated.

'We good?' Miles asked.

'Yes, Boss,' Jay replied grumpily.

'Fantastic, so stop feeling sorry for yourself like a little bitch and go sort it out. I'll be back after lunch. Don't ring me unless it's world-ending.'

Jay nodded, as Miles exited the office with his head in his phone. Miles was a hot head and he was a royal cunt at times, but Jay knew he'd pushed his buttons. If that had been any other boss, it wouldn't have been a show of strength, it would have been a bullet. Jay was dispensable and he knew it, but he also knew Miles only saved his skills for those who deserved it.

And God help anyone who deserved it.

Jay had heard about Romano; Lenny had rang to book the clean-up team. He squeezed his legs together just thinking about what Miles had done to him. Romano must have been well fucked up to earn a rusty nail through his balls. He shuddered still thinking about it. Although from what Lenny had said it hadn't been drawn out long.

Unlike Tweedle.

Just before all this shit with Joey started, Jay and Miles had realised small bits of shipments were going missing. So small most people wouldn't notice. Miles wasn't most people. Jay had placed men on the docks to keep tabs and Lenny had caught Tweedle red-handed, stealing bits of whatever he could sell for a quick fix. The punishment was definitely not quick.

Jay wasn't sure where Miles learnt to do what he did, but the piercing screams from Tweedle as Miles poured salt into the freshly open wound he had carved into his thighs were enough to remind everyone there that there was a reason Miles was feared.

There was no mercy, there was no remorse, there was just pain and Miles continued to take his payment in flesh, piece by piece, weighing each piece on a set of scales in front of Tweedle as he struggled to stay conscious in between the waves of pain. When Jay asked him why he'd weighed the pieces he'd carved out of him all he'd said was, 'The pound of flesh, which I demand is dearly bought: 'tis mine and I will have it.'

After a quick scan through Google, Jay found it was a quote from Shakespeare, *The Merchant of Venice*, where a money lender demanded his repayment in a pound of flesh when the merchant couldn't pay what he owed. Jay knew Miles was a fan of books, a secret few knew, but he'd never be as stupid to mention it to anyone else. It wouldn't help his rep.

Sitting back at his desk, Jay sighed. Miles was definitely not himself and he wasn't sure if it was the feisty redhead from the club or the pressure from Joey, but a distracted Miles was a dangerous thing. He was usually very logical and calculated, leaving nothing to chance, but the past few days things were... off.

They had still not had any leads on which gang was putting hits out on Joey's boys, Joey was breathing down their necks but doing fuck all to help and to top it off Miles was now rearranging meets they'd spent months planning. It wasn't even noon and he needed a drink.

'PIXIE!' Jay bellowed.

Pixie's small frame appeared in the doorway. 'Yes sir?'

'Can you grab me a drink please and check the rotas for tonight? I think two of the girls have called in sick, so we'll need cover.'

'Not a problem, sir, I'll get that sorted for you.'

'What would I do without you?' he sighed, head in his hands.

'I'm sure you'd be just fine without me, sir,' Pixie replied with a wink, leaving him with his thoughts.

Jay turned to his phone. He was not looking forward to rescheduling this meeting. He hoped whatever Miles had cancelled it for was worth it.

Eleven

He was already sitting waiting for her as she entered the small restaurant. She had agreed to lunch, not some fancy meal expensive enough to feed a small country.

Pandora hated wasted money, especially when it was wasted on showing off. That was just ego.

He stood with that smirk, the smirk that wouldn't have been there if he'd known the truth. But she'd played her part well for the most part and most men were too stubborn to think someone like her capable of anything... her greatest weapon.

'Pandora,' he stood pulling back a chair for her, 'I thought for a moment you were going to stand me up.'

'I'm sure that would have been a novel experience for you, Mr Wyatt,' she retorted, sitting as he pushed the chair in, returning to opposite her on the small cosy table.

'It's never happened yet, but there's always a first,' he chuckled. 'But what do I have to do to get you to call me Miles?'

'I get the impression most people don't call you Miles.' She paused. 'Okay, I'll call you Miles on one condition.' He nodded for her to continue. 'Tell me why we are here.'

'We're having lunch,' The statement was simple. The waiter appeared with two beautifully prepared plates. He'd taken the liberty of ordering for them both. Pandora eyed the plate and the beautifully crafted chicken and pasta dish before her. Lucky guess, she thought, twisting her fork in to take a bite.

'No. I mean why is it everywhere I turn, you appear? Are you stalking me?' she questioned between bites.

'No,' he chuckled running a hand through his short, slicked-back hair. 'You intrigue me, Pandora.'

She crossed her arms, leaning back, watching his expression. So, he didn't know anything about her, as far as she could tell, but why the interest?

'What,' she snorted, 'because I didn't fall into your arms or bed?'

'Maybe,' he paused taking his phone from his pocket as it buzzed. He took a glance at the screen and frowned. Pandora tried to see the caller ID but the screen wasn't in view and she wasn't about to blow everything yet.

'Excuse me one moment.' He stood, answering the phone as he walked away from the table, the disdain in his voice was clear. But who did he hate that much but would still take a call from them? Glancing around, she looked for an excuse to get closer but the bathrooms were in the opposite direction. She tapped her foot impatiently, knowing this wasn't going to be a quick route, but if Miles could lead her to Joey it would be worth the payoff.

'Sorry about that. Work.' He forced a small smile, as he returned to his seat. 'So where were we?'

'You were telling me how disappointed you were that I didn't fall into your bed,' she replied with a grin.

'No.'

'Oh really, so why are we here? Mr Miles...'

His jaw tensed, quickly replaced with a grin, he was ready to play the game.

'Just because you didn't, doesn't mean you won't. I've always liked a challenge, Pandora, and I think I've found one in you.'

An involuntary gulp escaped Pandora, her thighs clenching together as she battled with her composure. This was not part of the plan.

'Well,' she replied, 'I hope you're not a sore loser... Miles,' his name rolled off her tongue slowly as his eyes locked with her lips.

'I don't lose.'

His phone rang again as he cursed, looking at the ID. 'Yes, Jay? This better be important,' he snapped into the phone. 'Shit. Is she okay?' He waited silently. 'I'm on my way.'

She. That was the word that stuck in Pandora's head. *She.*

'Everything okay?' Pandora tried to pry.

'Pixie's been hurt, I need to go.' he actually sounded concerned.

'I'm coming with you.'

'No.'

'She's my friend. I'm coming.'

'Pandora, this isn't your world. You work in a bookshop. I'll make sure Pixie is okay and I'm sure she will ring you later. I'm sorry to cut our lunch short.' He stood, leaving without another word.

Waiting a few seconds until he was out of earshot, Pandora grabbed her phone.

'Frankie, something's happened to Pixie, I want to know everything.' The phone went dead. Ringing a second number she tapped her foot rapidly. 'Nora, tell the old boy I won't be back today. If anyone comes asking, I've gone home ill. And Nora, don't forget the gun is under the till in the drawer, make sure the safety is off before you shoot if you have to use it, just like you practised.'

Standing, Pandora called to pay the waiter but of course, the bill had already been settled in advance. Men! She dialled for a third time. 'Wayne, come grab me, we've got work to do. Meet me round the back.'

As she headed out of the restaurant, there was only one thing on Pandora's mind. Revenge. Joey was pushed to the back of her mind. Pixie was one of her own. Nobody got away with hurting one of her own. Nobody.

Twelve

'I know you said not to ring, Boss, but…' Jay stammered

'No, you were right to ring. Where is she?' Miles demanded, pushing past him.

'She's in here, she didn't want to go to hospital, so I got Doc out to sort her.' Jay led the way into the office.

Curled up on the couch was the tiny dot that was Pixie.

'Hey, Mr Wyatt,' she lifted herself with a shaky smile.

'Don't move too much, you need to rest,' Miles said and lay her back down, pulling a chair next to the couch.

Jay came over, Miles glared at him. 'What the fuck happened?' he demanded.

'She was downstairs setting up. I heard shots and came running down but the cars were already screeching away. I found her on the floor by the bar bleeding.' He paused, grabbing a remote. 'I've pulled up the footage.'

Turning their attention to the screen, they watched as the bar was stormed by seven figures, all masked up. They ran in, shooting everywhere. This wasn't a hit; it was a message and poor Pixie paid the price. Miles watched as she tried to take cover by the bar, a stray bullet catching her. The whole thing only lasted seconds, but it played in slow motion as they watched it over and over trying to look for clues.

Turning his attention back to Pixie, Miles looked at her injuries. Her shoulder was strapped and bandaged.

'It's okay, Mr Wyatt, it was straight through my shoulder. The doctor says I'll be fine to work in no time and I can always do back-of-house stuff 'til then so I don't put the customers off.'

'You will not be working!' he snapped, causing her to wince.

'But…' she protested.

'No arguing, you'll rest with full pay until you are fit to come back to work. Until then I'll have someone watch over you.'

'There's no need, Mr Wyatt, honestly I'll be fine. I just want to go home and sleep if that's okay?'

'Of course. I'll take you home.'

Her eyes widened. 'I can get a taxi, it's no bother, honestly.'

'It's not up for debate Pixie. You may want to ring your friend Pandora though, I think she was worried. But, Pixie, no telling her our business… understand?'

Pixie nodded. The message was clear. She looked around for her phone. Jay handed her the battered phone and the screen lit up. It still worked. Lifting herself up, she dialled.

'Hey Pan, it's me… Yes, I'm fine,' Pixie paused glancing at the two men towering over her. 'Mr Wyatt is going to take me home… Yes, I just need some sleep.' The phone line went dead.

Carefully lifting Pixie into his arms, still holding her phone, Miles carried her effortlessly through the club and out to the car, followed by Jay with her bag. Placing her in the front passenger seat he gently put her seatbelt around her and took the bag from Jay placing it on her lap.

'Get the place cleaned up and ready for tonight. Call in whoever you need, but we open on time. Understand?'

Jay nodded.

'And find out who the fuck did this. I want them. Alive.' He gritted his teeth.

The ride was silent apart from the low buzz of the radio filling the background. Pixie dozed in and out of sleep as Miles glanced at her occasionally. She worked for him, she was his responsibility. This was his fault. Miles didn't let anyone hurt what was his. He gripped his wheel tighter.

As they pulled into Pixie's apartment block, Miles unclicked her belt, exiting round to her side of the car and lifting her out.

'Mr Wyatt, my legs are fine. I can walk.'

'Shush, you need to rest.'

He carried her to her battered door, setting her down softly so she could get her key from her bag. Opening the door, she headed inside. She didn't fully open the door, but he glimpsed the bare

41

apartment inside. She didn't have much by the looks of it. Did she live alone?

'Thank you, Mr Wyatt. For everything,' she said with a small smile.

'Ring me if you need anything Pixie, I'll have one of the guys pop by to check on you later.'

Her face dropped and he took it as a sign of fear. 'Don't worry, Pixie, you're safe, we'll make sure of it.'

She nodded palely, closing the door and bolting it shut as he headed off. As she turned, a figure emerged from the corner of the room.

'Boss! Wasn't expecting you to be here already.'

Pandora crossed the room examining the bandaged shoulder as Pixie cringed.

'Who?'

'Joey's boys,' Pixie sighed. 'They all had the neck tattoo. It was them.'

'Did you tell him?'

'No, but I think he'll work it out soon enough.'

'Why the fuck is Joey shooting out Wyatt's place?'

'I think I know,' Pixie interrupted. 'I was listening in to Jay's phone calls earlier. Joey is forcing Miles to find out who's hitting his shipments and taking out his crews. Joey isn't happy with the lack of answers, I think this was a warning.'

So, Miles wasn't working with Joey, he was being forced to do his dirty work. Pandora hadn't taken Miles as the type to do anything he didn't want to…

'We need to find out what Joey has over Miles,' said Pandora.

'Well, I'm out of action. Mr Wyatt has told me I can't work 'til I'm better, I'm off with full pay.'

'Alright for some,' Pandora teased, seeing a blush creep into Pixie's cheeks. Pandora was torn on her opinion of Miles Wyatt. A ruthless killer, who takes her to lunch, drives Pixie home and gives her full pay? No, he was a monster, just like the rest of them. She couldn't forget that. She couldn't lose sight of the goal.

Justice.

Thirteen

A week had passed. There had been no more shipments, no more shootouts and it was quiet. Too quiet.

Pandora stood in the VIP section overlooking the dance floor of Limbo. Frankie and Pixie sat chattering quietly behind her.

She was getting restless, she needed to calm herself and focus, this was all about the long game. That would require patience.

Frankie drew Pandora's attention, responding to a call in her earpiece. 'Yes Seb, you know what to do,' she replied standing and walking to Pandora.

'Boss, we have a visitor,' she nodded to the entrance.

Pandora groaned as she saw who had just walked into her club. Miles Wyatt.

He was accompanied by a group of men and women, with a peroxide blonde glued to his arm. Frankie nudged Pan playfully. 'Looks like your new boyfriend's cheating on you, Boss.'

The glare was all Frankie needed to shut up. Pan assessed the group; they were all his own lot plus the female companions. It wasn't unusual for gangs to frequent her establishments; they were neutral ground. She'd never been concerned about visitors before. Well, not before her run-in with Miles Wyatt. Pandora's grip tightened on the balcony as the underdressed blonde whispered into Miles's ear. She watched him grin. She glared towards the blonde, before realising the emotions that were teasing her. She did not give a fuck about Miles Wyatt; he was merely a means to an end. As if sensing the glare in his direction, he looked up, his eyes locking with hers. He immediately dropped his arm from around his companion's waist, a smirk arising as he excused himself from his companions, heading in her direction.

'You going to dip, Boss?' Frankie enquired.

'No that would look too suspicious, we'll let this play out. You know what to do.'

Frankie cued her radio. 'All teams, code 4, please be advised we are on code 4.'

Pandora stepped back from the balcony, seating herself between Pixie and Frankie.

As Miles reached the edge of the VIP area, Nate stepped in his way. 'Sorry sir this area is reserved for VIP only.'

Miles glared at the oversized brute, he wasn't in his own playground today. He needed to play nice. He spied Pixie sitting with Pandora and another young lady with a stylish-looking eye patch.

'Of course my good man, I don't suppose you could ask the young ladies if I could join them for a moment? Two of them are acquaintances of mine.'

Nate looked back at the ladies, but it was Frankie who responded. 'Let the gentleman in Nate.' Nate nodded allowing Miles to pass as he approached with a grin.

'Pixie, I'm glad to see you're up and about. I hope you're not overdoing it,' he smiled in her direction.

'Hi Mr Wyatt, no I'm getting lots of rest, but Pandora thought I could use a break as I was going a bit stir crazy, so we came to see our friend Frankie. She's the manager here.' Pixie gestured to Frankie who stood, extending a hand.

'Mr Wyatt, nice to have you in our club, I hope you enjoy your evening.'

'I think I definitely will now with such good company.' He paused. 'You know who I am?'

'I know who most people are, sir, comes with the job,' she replied with a grin.

Pandora interrupted. 'Shouldn't you be getting back to your date, Mr Miles?' she asked with a sharp undertone.

'Not getting jealous are we, Pandora?' he teased. 'I thought you didn't drink?'

She raised her glass. 'No, I just said I didn't drink with you, Mr Wyatt.'

'Well, I'm sure we can change that. Why don't you come and join us?'

'Wouldn't want to upset your date,' Pandora smirked.

'Date? Oh, you mean Ciara? She's not my date, she's my little sister. It's her birthday.'

A wave flashed over Pandora, but before she could reply, Frankie stood up clapping.

'Well, we can't keep the birthday girl waiting, can we? Let's show her how Limbo treats its guests in true VIP style.'

Pandora sighed. This was going to get messy.

Fourteen

A wave of energy spread throughout the club as the bass pumped. Frankie beckoned over one of the hosts to the booth she had led the group to.

'Lilith, these are my personal guests tonight, so make sure you give them the VIP treatment.'

The tall, slender blonde nodded, retreating off behind the bar.

Pixie and Pandora stood on the edge of the booth area. Pandora could see Pixie looked slightly on edge when one of Wyatt's group approached her.

'Pixie! How are you feeling?' he shouted grinning.

'I'm much better, Jay, I'll be back at work in no time,' she replied, trying to raise her voice loud enough so he could hear.

'Fantastic, we are missing you at the club. It isn't the same without you.'

Pixie blushed and Pandora noticed the almost sincere tone in his voice, but she wasn't fooled. Trust was something you couldn't afford to gift to the wrong person. He turned his attention to Pandora.

'So you must be the elusive Pandora,' he smirked. Pandora, hand on her right hip, raised an eyebrow as he continued. 'You must be something special to have the Boss so distracted.'

She wasn't sure if it was a compliment or an accusation. But she remained silent, the buzz about him from the alcohol might loosen his lips but she didn't want to push and draw any suspicion. As she was about to move in, the birthday girl approached, interrupting.

'Hi, I'm Ciara,' she extended a hand excitedly.

'Pan, pleased to meet you,' she engaged in the shake, before being pulled into a non-consensual hug.

Ciara seemed sweet and Pandora almost regretted her initial harsh judgement. Close up the girl was in fact a natural blonde, very beautiful, with quite an innocent vibe around her.

'Miles never usually lets me come out to clubs with him, but he said this one was the best in town. He's just such an overprotective big brother,' she whinged, giggling.

Pandora knew the reason. Limbo was neutral ground which everyone believed to be run by Frankie for a foreign wealthy investor with no gang connections, nobody would target another gang there. He was keeping her out of his world it would seem, either that or she was in for an Oscar.

'Would you like to come dance?' she blurted out.

'I don't really dance. I'm sure one of the lads will dance with you, or one of the girls?' Pandora diverted, nodding at the group who were currently downing shots.

'Nah, they are too scared of my brother, the big pussy cat that he is, and the girls I don't know, they just came with my brother's mates. I think you're more my kind of fun! Come on, us girls can show 'em how it's done,' she squealed, bouncing in her heels, pulling Pandora and Pixie to the dance floor as an amused Frankie tried to keep her composure from the sidelines.

Pandora knew she had to play along, but she had a reputation to uphold. Fuck it. Sacrifices must be made. Grabbing a shot off a passing host she downed the burning liquid.

Ciara let loose on the dancefloor and Pixie joined in immediately, but Pandora held back, scanning the club. Ciara was already attracting a lot of attention from the male patrons, but a few discreet glances to the boys on security and they were diverted away by hostesses and dancers tempting them with free shots. They didn't need a blood bath tonight if the wrong person hit on Miles Wyatt's baby sister.

The DJ raised an eyebrow at Pandora and, with the corner of her lip turning upwards, adjusted her headphones. Pandora glared back. Lila looked good as a brunette and with the additional tattoos she'd acquired over the last week, she was re-invented. Pan had almost laughed when Lila said she'd always wanted to be a DJ but after reluctantly letting her near the decks she realised Lila had it on lock, she could hold a club in the palm of her hand.

47

After a whisper in her ear from one of the hosts, Lila picked up the mic.

'We have a very special guest in the house tonight! The birthday girl Ciara is ripping it up on the dance floor! You go girl!'

Ciara's eyes lit up at the surprise, the joy clear as she continued swaying her hips against Pixie, who was a natural on the dancefloor.

'Didn't see you as much of a dancer,' the voice came from behind Pandora. She didn't need to turn to know who it was.

'I'm not, but your sister was relentless,' Pandora groaned.

'Yeah, she is pretty persistent. She seems to like you and Pixie though. It's not often she talks to people she doesn't know,' he sighed looking at Ciara as she spun carefree in front of them.

'Is that by her choice or yours?' Pan snapped, instantly regretting the comment.

Two strong arms spun her around. Hands firmly on her upper arms. No smile present.

'I take the safety of those I care about very seriously.'

'You run a nightclub, Mr Wyatt, it's not like you're part of the bloody mafia,' she was treading a thin line here and she knew it, but her patience was wearing thin and she needed something, anything.

His hands dropped, quickly replacing the stone face with a small smile.

'I suppose you're right. But she is my little sister, I'm sure you can understand.'

Ciara may not have been winning any Oscars, but Miles Wyatt definitely was. The way he could lie so effortlessly and not even betray a hint of the life he hid was almost impressive.

A grin crept onto his face. Pan could see he was up to something. Before she could calculate her next move, he had spun her back around, hands firmly on her hips, swaying in time with the beats. Before she could protest, her eyes met with Pixie and Ciara, one shocked, one grinning. Every part of her body tensed as she fought the urge to push him away. This is what got her into this mess in the first place. If she had just kept her head down and not made eye contact, this would never have got to this stage.

He rested his head on her shoulder as he continued to sway to the music, leading her hips in synch with his. In any other life, with any other guy, this could have been something she might have enjoyed. But she couldn't, she wouldn't.

This was not how the night was supposed to go.

Fifteen

When Ciara eventually slowed down enough to be led off the dance floor, they returned to the booth where Lilith was waiting with drinks. Pandora nodded, taking a glass. Lilith went to open her mouth but then stopped, excusing herself she headed back to the bar. She'd nearly slipped, but she'd caught herself just in time.

Frankie headed back over to the booth.

'I hope you're all enjoying your evening,' she smiled.

'Yes, thank you for the hospitality and good company,' Miles replied toasting his glass towards Pandora and Pixie, who were sat opposite him with Ciara.

Frankie sat down between Pandora and Miles, much to his annoyance.

'I'm surprised to see you out though, Mr Wyatt, I thought you'd be busy with your own clubs on a night like tonight,' Frankie chuckled.

'Yes, well. Family first and Ciara deserved to have a good birthday. Least I could for my little sister.'

Ciara blushed.

Frankie's probing wasn't working. She wasn't really the subtle interrogator and it was obvious Miles wasn't attracted to her or any other girl, to be honest. If it hadn't been for him pursuing Pandora she would have thought his interests lay elsewhere.

'I was equally surprised,' he interrupted, 'to see Pandora here.'

Pandora's eyes locked with his, seeing where this was going.

'I didn't think you were the nightclub type.'

'I'm not. Pixie needed to get out and Frankie was kind enough to invite us over. Would have been rude not to.' She paused. 'Speaking of Pixie, any news on the culprits who tried to rob your club? I'm

not sure I feel comfortable with my friend being there if she's in…
danger.'

He put his drink down.

'They've been dealt with.'

Pandora knew it was bullshit but she couldn't call him out on it, not yet.

Lilith appeared right on cue with yet another tray of shots. Pandora took the clear one closest. Ciara took the Goldschläger with the sparkly stars in it and the rest were shared amongst the group who were getting tipsier by the minute.

They had a higher tolerance for alcohol than Pandora would have liked, Frankie was going to moan about the stock loss, but this was more important than a few hundred on complimentary drinks in the grand scheme of things.

Miles had headed to the toilet when Jay plonked himself down between Pixie and Pandora, he was definitely leaning to the side of drunk.

'Pixie, I miss you so much at work, it's so dull without you.'

Pixie blushed.

'But you,' he said pointing at Pandora, 'you're dangerous.'

She paused, waiting for the implosion.

'You,' he continued waving his finger, 'You are a distraction and you're going to get the Boss killed.'

'What do you mean?' Pandora asked, she wasn't sure where this was going but this was definitely the break she needed tonight.

'I think someone has had too much to drink,' came an annoyed voice from behind them.

Jay's back straightened and he looked like an ice bucket had just been tipped over his head. Quickly backtracking, he tried to explain.

'Boss man here nearly fell down the stairs trying to look at you, you need to come with a hazard warning!' he chuckled. Smooth, thought Pan, but not smooth enough.

The glare from Miles faded slightly, but she could still see the annoyance there. Something was going on and it definitely involved her. That couldn't be good. Joey didn't know about their interactions, did he? No, she would have heard something. She needed eyes and ears back in that club ASAP. Pixie needed to go back to work.

A retching noise pulled everyone's attention. Ciara's blonde hair was being gently held back by Pixie as she puked into the nearest champagne bucket. *Oh well, at least it wasn't the floor*, thought Pan.

Miles rolled his eyes as he slid round the booth, lifting his sister's arm around his shoulder as another male got the other side. Gently they walked her to the exit. Pandora's shoulders relaxed slightly as the group followed out, thanking Frankie for her hospitality.

As Pandora went to head to the office, she saw Miles re-enter the club. She diverted from the office as if she were going to the bathroom.

'Thought you'd gone?' she asked as he approached.

'Wouldn't be much of a gentleman if I left without saying bye.'

'Who said you were a gentleman?'

'Ouch,' he grabbed his chest playfully, 'that hurt!'

Pandora smiled at his stupidity.

'Thank you for being nice to my sister tonight, she really had a good time.'

'She's a nice girl...' Pandora paused.

'What, unlike her brother?' Miles teased.

'Definitely,' Pandora replied. This was becoming too easy, the words were just rolling off her tongue.

'So, I ran out on our lunch, can I make it up to you?'

'No need.' She needed to keep some distance; this was getting into murky waters way too quickly.

'Please,' his face softened, almost begging her to submit.

'I'll think about it.'

'I'll take that as a work in progress,' he grinned like a small child, walking away, 'good night, Pandora.'

'Goodnight Mr Wyatt.'

Sixteen

It wasn't as simple as good and evil, Pandora had learnt that lesson early on. One of many lessons. The second was when it came to life you were either looking down the barrel of a gun or looking up one. She had decided long ago she would never be looking up one again.

She'd been waiting for an update from Frankie for over an hour. She didn't like being kept waiting. Tonight came with risks, but there was no avoiding it. Everyone was radio silent tonight, but she should have been back by now.

Her heels echoed as she paced.

'Something's not right,' she said to nobody in particular. They'd done this numerous times before. It was always meticulously planned. There was nothing that should go wrong but the danger was always there. Her gut was telling her tonight was the night it would not go to plan.

To the world, she was fearless and ruthless.

They didn't know her name.

They didn't know her face. Heck, they didn't even know she wasn't a man.

She had built an empire from the shadows and she wasn't scared of getting her hands dirty. In fact, she quite liked it, probably a little too much. But she was smart and she knew that this game had to be played in secret. Too much was at stake to let pride or adrenaline get in the way.

Car tyres screeched outside the warehouse and Pandora sped towards the doors. Stepping outside she saw four black cars pull up.

Pandora let out a breath but stopped again when she saw Frankie getting out of the front passenger seat holding her arm.

The blood was trickling through her fingers and down her hand as it gripped tightly.

'It's fine, Boss, just a graze before you start getting all mushy on me,' Frankie teased with a grin.

Pandora stormed up to her, punching her in her good arm.

'Ouch! What was that for?'

'What the fuck happened?'

'It was a trap. They were waiting for us.'

'And you walked right into it?'

'Well yeah, I wasn't leaving without them,' Frankie nodded to the cars behind her, watching as Seb, Wayne and the others were helping shaky figures out of the cars. Women. No, not women; girls. All wide-eyed and tremoring as the boys helped them out and towards the warehouse. She clenched her fists as she watched, knowing the helpless fear each one of them was feeling. Knowing that the nightmare they had lived would stay with them in their sleep for the rest of their lives.

Pandora watched on as Wayne carried a small figure into the warehouse, mousy brown hair and dark chocolate eyes. She had dirt all over her face as she was clenching tightly onto a teddy bear. She couldn't have been more than eight.

'As I said, Boss,' interrupted Frankie, 'I wasn't leaving without them.' The grit and determination on Frankie's face was clear. Pan knew she would have done the same in that situation.

Pandora nodded to her. She counted nine in total. Goodness knows how many had started out on the journey.

Everyone got to work settling the girls; grabbing blankets, bottles of water and chocolate bars to hand out. Seb began to patch up Frankie and Nate who had been shot in the leg, both grumbling about not needing help. As Pandora surveyed the girls, she came to the youngest that Wayne had carried in.

'Hey there, what's your name?' Pandora asked with a soft smile.

'My name's Izzy.'

'That's a lovely name Izzy, I love your teddy bear, does he have a name too?'

Izzy shook her head, 'He's not mine.'

'Oh,' said Pandora confused.

'He belongs to the man,' Izzy continued.

'What man Izzy?' Pandora urged.

'The man with the tattoo on his neck. He said I had to keep it with me 'til he came and got it.'

'May I have a look?' Pandora reached her hand out and Izzy passed her the bear. It was brand new, not a mark on it, unlike the small child who was filthy.

'FUCK!' shouted Pandora.

The room stopped.

'We've been set up! We need to go. NOW!' she screamed.

Before anyone could move they heard the tyres screeching on the gravel outside.

They were fucked.

Seventeen

The evidence was clear. Joey's boys had hit Temptation and hurt Pixie, all to send a fucking message; that Joey didn't like waiting. Joey had pushed too far this time. This couldn't be overlooked.

Miles couldn't be seen to be weak; he might as well put a gun to his head and pull the trigger himself if he did. But going against Joey was just as dangerous. Joey had nothing over Miles as such, but Miles had promised his father not to go against him.

'Joey is like family Miles; you must respect him.' Miles remembered the lecture from his father.

'But he doesn't respect me!' Miles would groan.

'Respect must be earned my boy and at the very least if you can't respect him, fear him. It will keep you, your mother and your sister alive.'

The warning was clear, don't mess with Joey. Up until this point Miles had respected his father's requests even though Joey wasn't even blood. But his mother was halfway around the world on some beach and his sister was never left unwatched.

Jay stormed into the office interrupting his thoughts.

'Ah Jay, I just about to call you.'

'Boss, I have news.'

'Yes, yes, but first I want you to arrange a holiday for Ciara. Don't arouse any suspicion, just send her somewhere fancy and far away and tell her it's a late birthday present.'

'Boss, that's what I'm trying to tell you. Ciara is gone!'

The air disappeared and Miles clutched his chest, taking a moment to focus. Clenching his fist, he smashed it down on his desk. He grabbed his phone and dialled.

'Yes…?'

'Where the fuck is she?'

Joey's slimy voice chuckled down the phone. 'Don't worry my boy, I'm taking good care of her. Let's just call her my new friend.'

'Joey, if you fucking…'

'You'll do what? Nothing. That's what. I own your ass just like I own hers. If I find out you've got anything to do with my shipments, I'll make sure you get a front-row seat to what I'm going to do to her. As long as you behave, I promise I'll be… gentle with her.'

Miles could hear Ciara's whimpering down the phone. He growled. 'I had nothing to do with your fucking shipments, she has nothing to do with this Joey. Let her go.'

'No, I think not. You've been getting too disobedient since your father passed and I think it's time you learnt your place. I think it's time you all remembered who is in charge.'

Joey hung up. Miles threw the phone across the room, smashing it and the mirror it collided with to pieces.

A gasp escaped from beyond the office door.

'Pixie…' Miles snapped, 'What the fuck are you doing?'

Jay opened the door, beckoning her in.

'I'm sorry for listening in, I didn't mean to, I don't usually say anything but I really like Ciara and I think I might know someone who can help. But first I need your help.'

Miles rounded in, closing the office door and backing Pixie against it.

'Boss…' Jay tried to reason.

'Shut up Jay,' Miles snapped, his eyes locked with Pixie's as he reached under the back of his jacket pulling out the gun and placing it against Pixie's head. Pixie, still meek, still shaking, didn't flinch at the touch of the metal as he applied pressure.

'Pixie. Talk. But don't think I won't fucking blow your brains out if I think you had something to do with my sister. If you are working for Joey, I will kill you.'

'No, you've got it wrong Mr Wyatt. I work for you, I've been loyal to you, I swear. But I have a friend who can help you. But first I need you to help them. I think they are in danger.'

Tightening his free hand around her throat, he applied pressure.

'Stop fucking with me Pixie. Tell me what the fuck is going on.'

'Boss! She can't breathe. This is Pixie for fuck's sake; Pixie. She was shot by Joey's boys, why would she be working for them?' Jay tried to reason with him.

He still didn't release her or his gaze. 'Joey's never minded collateral damage before, he could have done it to keep doubt off her. We know how persuasive he can be.'

'Mr Wyatt,' Pixie choked out between breaths, 'we're running out of time. Please... Think of Ciara.'

He released his grip and lowering his gun, he took a step back, releasing her.

'Talk.'

'My friend,' Pixie stammered. 'My friend can help you get your sister back. But I think they are in danger and I need your help before it's too late for all of us. We need to hurry!'

'You screw me over Pixie and you'll regret it. Understood?'

Pixie nodded, knowing this was a gamble but without any other tricks up her sleeve.

Eighteen

'Fuck, Fuck, Fuck!' Pandora paced back and forth. They had the front surrounded and without the cars, they wouldn't make it far. But what were they waiting for? If it were the other way round, she would have stormed the place, killing everyone in it.

They were waiting for Joey.

Shit.

Phone signal was crap – she couldn't ring out – she'd tried sending a message to Lila and Pixie but she had no way of knowing if it had gotten through and even then, there wasn't enough time for them to get there with enough backup. She'd still be exposed. Joey would know it was her. He'd start to put everything together.

Everything she'd sacrificed, everything she'd fought for. All thrown away because she'd been too soft. She looked down at Izzy, still clutching the bear. She knew if she had her time over, she'd do it all again.

Too fucking right.

The girls were all crying, even the younger ones because they knew what was waiting outside. They thought they'd been saved. Frankie looked around awkwardly; she wasn't really the maternal figure. Seb seemed to be doing a better job trying to calm them, he was a big teddy bear when he wasn't torturing or killing people. Wayne hopped down from his vantage point.

'What we looking at?' Pandora asked.

'There's twelve that I can count Boss. We could take them but no guarantee there wouldn't be collateral.' Wayne glanced at the girls behind Pandora. 'We may not have a choice though.'

'Fuck that,' Pandora spat. 'It's the one thing that keeps us apart from dirt like them. There is no such thing as expendable lives.'

She knew he was right though; they were running out of options.

'We haven't got much time, Boss, they are obviously waiting for backup.'

'They are waiting for him.'

'You think he would come himself, Boss?'

'Yes,' she grimaced, 'he'll want to do the deed himself for the amount of money I've cost him.'

'*We've* cost him, Boss. You're not alone in this,' Wayne reassured her.

As Pandora looked around the room, she saw the steely resolve in each of her team. All with their own reasons for being there, but all with a debt to repay. To her. She had saved each of them in one way or another. If she was going down, she was taking as many of the fuckers down with her.

Decision made.

'Get the girls to the back,' she barked. 'Use whatever you can to build a barrier to keep them out of the firing line.'

Everyone started moving and some of the older girls who had stopped crying started helping too. These were survivors, these were warriors, they just didn't know it yet. She knew their fear, she knew their pain and she knew how strong they truly were underneath all the trauma.

She had been them.

There was movement outside.

They'd run out of time.

Signalling to Nate, Wayne and Frankie, Pandora sent them to higher vantage points. Grabbing weapons, they settled themselves as high as they could.

Pandora, Seb and the others spread themselves out, the last line of defence. A voice came from behind her.

'We can help too,' one of the older girls whispered. Brunette. Covered in cuts and bruises, her tear-stained face met Pandora's. Three other girls all stood nodding.

'You need as much help as you can get,' she bargained, 'let us help.'

Pandora didn't want to put children in the firing line, but these girls had long stopped being children.

'Seb, grab them a weapon, show them how to use the safety, point and shoot.'

The girls nodded at Pandora before Seb grabbed four guns, showing the girls the fast-track guide on how to use them. The guns looked so heavy in the girls' hands, but none of them shrank back. Pandora remembered the first time she'd felt the weight of a gun in her hands, the kickback the first time she'd fired and the look of life leaving another human being's eyes as she shot him. He wasn't a human being, she'd told herself. Human beings didn't do what these men had done.

She had slept soundly that night. She wasn't sure the girls would, but there were far worse nightmares than taking the life of someone who thoroughly deserved it.

A shot rang out.

'Boss, you're not going to believe what I'm seeing!' Wayne shouted from his perch.

'It can't be!' Frankie gasped.

'What the fuck is going on?' shouted Pandora.

Before anyone could explain, shots erupted outside the warehouse. Shouting and confusion followed. The younger girls sobbed as the older ones tried to calm them.

Pandora still hadn't got a fucking clue what was going on. Bracing herself, she, Seb and the others took aim, steading themselves ready for the breach. Her heart was pumping, if it hadn't been for the girls in the firing line behind her, she'd almost be excited for the chance to try and shoot Joey. If she survived long enough.

Wayne, Frankie and Nate had started shooting, but Pandora had yet to hear a shot returned in their direction.

She spoke too soon. Bullets were hitting the outside of the warehouse. Wayne, Frankie and Nate were all well-hidden, using small windows and gaps to shoot through. But it was only a matter of time before Joey's boys got through.

Had Joey arrived with backup?

Nineteen

As they pulled up to the docks, Miles still didn't have the answers he wanted. Pixie had promised him her friend could get Ciara back but he still hadn't got a clue who this friend was or what trouble they were in.

The docks were Miles's territory, he rented out warehouses and storage and controlled what came in and out of the port. Pixie assured him this was where her friend would be.

As they approached the docks, one of the guards ran up to the car.

'Mr Wyatt!' he shouted, 'I'm so glad you're here, I was just about to ring you. I mean there's something not right.'

'Will you just tell me what the fuck you're trying to tell me? I'm in a rush.'

The man stopped and took a breath. 'There's something happening down by warehouse 7 sir, lots of cars. I think some of them are Mr Siegel's boys but the first lot weren't. Just thought you should know.'

'Mr Wyatt,' Pixie whispered, 'Warehouse 7 is where my friend is, we're too late.'

'How long ago?' Miles asked the guard.

'Mr Siegel's lot turned up about five minutes ago, the first lot about twenty minutes before that. It's been silent down there since.'

No gunfire yet then, thought Miles. Gesturing the guard to give him his radio Miles changed to channel 3.

'Lenny, you there?'

'Yes, Boss,' came the gruff reply.

'Warehouse 9 behind warehouse 7 now. Grab the team, meet me there, stocked up.'

'On the way.'

Miles turned back to the guard, 'Lock down the port, nobody else gets in. You understand? Nobody.'

The guard gulped, nodding before grabbing another radio and racing off.

Jay turned off the lights and they drove slowly down the path, turning left and then taking the third right. A large warehouse with the number 9 came into sight. A group of grouchy-looking men were already standing waiting.

All armed. All ready.

Miles, Jay and Pixie all hopped out of the car.

Lenny approached Miles, dropping a bag to the floor. Jay knelt down, unzipping it and passing Miles a gun before grabbing one for himself. Pixie edged in closer, reaching into the bag.

'Pixie what are you doing?' asked Jay.

'I'm coming with you,' she replied bluntly. No shyness, no stammer. She picked up the gun, checked it was loaded, slid it into the back of her belt and stood.

Miles watched as she handled herself with a confidence he had never seen before. It radiated off her. This wasn't the first time she'd handled a gun. What else did he not know about his little Pixie?

'We will talk about this later Pixie; this conversation is not over.'

'Yes sir,' she replied with a salute.

'Who are you and what have you done with Pixie?' Jay interrupted.

'Jay we don't have time for this,' snapped Miles. Jay nodded.

They approached warehouse 7 on foot, silent and careful not to arouse suspicion. As they got closer, Miles could hear voices.

'Boss man said not to move 'til he gets here. He wants to see the fuckers burn himself,' the first voice demanded.

'What about the girls they took?' the other voice replied.

'He said it's worth the loss, let them burn too. They were only the bait. He's got another shipment due in any day.'

Miles signalled to Lenny. Lenny in turn signalled to his boys who fanned out at a distance. Pixie and Jay stayed close to Miles.

'Your friend better be able to get my sister back,' Miles threatened, 'If we do this now, we start a war, you know that don't you?'

'And you'll be on the right side Mr Wyatt,' replied Pixie flatly. She pulled out her gun, taking off the safety.

Miles nodded to Lenny and several pops were heard.

Joey's boys now knew they were under attack. Shots rained freely. Miles and Jay took refuge behind the nearest car, shooting and ducking. Lenny and the boys were spread out, locked in firefights with the enemy.

Miles glanced up as he saw Pixie take out a blond-haired brute that was creeping up on Lenny, no hesitation, no flinch, not even a blink as she shot him in the back up the head, casually wiping the blood off of her face before moving on.

Shots came from the top of the warehouse. They were under fire! They were getting shot at by the fuckers they were trying to help!

A bullet shot past Pixie, taking out the guy to her left who'd been closing in. She blew a kiss in the direction the bullet had come from.

The shots coming from the warehouse weren't aiming for them! They were hitting Joey's boys. Joey's boys were getting hit from both sides and the confusion was clear.

Miles spotted one crouched down by a nearby car talking on a phone.

'Boss! We've been ambushed, we're getting hit from all sides. You have to...'

He hit the ground before the sentence was complete, Lenny towering over him before stamping on the phone.

Silence took over.

A single shot rang out. Miles looked up to see Pixie over a groaning figure. She shot again, but she still didn't kill him.

'We should keep at least one alive,' she reasoned, 'we may need information and he has one of Joey's inner tattoos.'

'You fucking bitch! I'm going to fucking kill you' the man screamed.

Pixie smiled, 'No you're not, but if I'm feeling nice, I might kill you before I chop your dick off and force you to give yourself a blow job.' She winked at him, blowing him a kiss before walking off without a care in the world towards the warehouse.

Lenny and Jay stood speechless.

'Boss,' Jay stammered.

'I don't have a fucking clue, Jay,' replied Miles.

Lenny beckoned over the lads and they followed behind Miles and Jay, who in turn were just behind Pixie.

As Pixie reached the doors, Miles placed a hand on her shoulder.

'Your friend better be worth this.'

Pixie smiled nervously, reaching out to open the warehouse doors.

'You better be worth this Mr Miles. You don't know the risk I've taken tonight.'

Twenty

The shots had stopped, but before Pandora could get answers from Wayne or Frankie there was movement at the door.

Pandora prepped her gun ready.

'Boss wait!' shouted Frankie.

Pandora hesitated for just a second, as Wayne, Frankie and Nate raced down, just as the door was opening.

Pixie!

Pandora's heart jumped when she saw Pixie's blood-stained face as she waltzed in but froze when she realised who was behind her.

'Pixie. What have you done?' Pandora whispered.

Two sets of eyes met. Shock, silence, questions.

'You,' they both said simultaneously.

'Boss, I'm sorry,' pleaded Pixie, 'I didn't know what else to do. I was at the club when I got your message and then I found out that Joey's taken Ciara. So, I took a risk.'

'You,' Miles glared. 'No. It can't be.'

He stared at the woman, fire in her eyes, gun still in her hand. His body twitched, conflicted. What other surprises would the night bring? Behind her, he noticed several figures. Big brutes guarding crying young girls and four shaky but fierce-looking girls holding guns they clearly didn't know how to use.

She ignored him, rounding in on Pixie. 'Joey took Ciara?' Pandora repeated, Pixie nodded.

'Can anyone tell me what fucked up dream I walked into?' Jay blurted out, 'I mean hot chicks with guns, I'm not complaining but I'm still confused,' he smirked, glancing at Frankie who threw him the finger.

Miles looked at Frankie. So much for just a nightclub manager.

'Pixie, I want answers!' he demanded.

'And you'll get them,' Pandora interrupted, 'but first we get these girls out of here.'

'And who,' he paused, towering over her, 'do you think you are, giving me orders Pandora?'

She took a step closer, their bodies now touching, looking up at him. 'I'm the one that can help you get your sister back,' she smiled, 'and you never know, you might like taking orders from me, Mr Miles.'

She stood back, her pulse racing as he stood there, mouth open, breath shallow.

'We'll see about that Pandora. This conversation isn't over.'

Pandora glanced over at Pixie who was currently being manhandled by Seb who was insistent on checking her from head to toe, to make sure she was okay.

'I'm fine Seb, it's not my blood. It's his,' she pointed over at the bleeding mess Lenny had dragged inside.

'I thought he might come in use later, Boss,' Pixie said addressing Pandora. She nodded.

Miles's eyes shot up as she addressed her. Boss. So, she worked for Pandora. The questions were stacking up fast. His eyes darted around, the respect she commanded from everyone in the room was clear.

'Right, we need to get out of here,' Pandora raised her voice. 'Mr Miles, since this is your turf, what's the best route out without Joey tracking us?'

'Service road behind warehouse 10,' Miles replied. 'It's not on maps and I don't tell anyone about it. That's our best bet.'

'Okay, let's get the girls loaded up and get out of here. Pixie, send Mr Miles the address.'

Pixie nodded, tapping away on her phone and Miles felt the ping on his. Who was she to be barking out orders at him? He went to speak but she ignored him, shouting orders to the others, splitting the girls up into smaller groups and setting her team up with each of them. He watched as she knelt down to the smallest child.

'Izzy,' she spoke softly, 'I think we should leave the bear here so the man can get it back and I'll buy you a nice new one of your own, is that okay?' The little girl nodded as Pandora took the bear off her. She reached into a bag one of her men was holding and took out a grenade. The goddamn woman had a grenade in her bag. Miles didn't know whether to be shocked or impressed.

'Go. I'll catch up,' she ordered to her team.

Miles turned to his team. 'Lenny, you, Jay and Sparky come with us, bring him too,' he gestured to the man Pixie had maimed. 'The others stay here and sort this out,' Lenny nodded.

'He's mine,' Pandora snapped.

'Learn to share your toys, Pan,' Miles winked. He wasn't giving her all the power in this.

Everyone headed out to the cars except Miles and Pandora. They stood silently. He watched as she carefully took the pin out of the grenade, placing it in the teddy bear and putting it down delicately on the chair. 'You've got insurance I'm sure,' she smirked.

Miles groaned, grabbing his radio.

'Keep everyone away from warehouse 7. That's an order.'

A flurry of responses came in reply, acknowledging.

'You coming, Mr Miles?' she asked playfully.

He frowned, following her out to the car where Jay and Pixie were waiting, the tension clear as they all got in the car. Jay and Pixie in the front, Miles and Pandora in the back. Pixie put the address in for Jay and the engine roared as they drove away from the warehouse.

Pandora took out her phone, dialling.

'Lila, yes I know. Things didn't go quite to plan. Yes, the girls are all fine. Wake Felix up and be ready for us. We've got some extra friends with us too. Yes, I'll explain when I get there. Have a teddy bear ready too, we've got a young'un.'

The phone call ended and Miles and Pandora sat staring out of opposite windows silently. Pixie didn't dare put the radio on. She was still waiting for the bollocking and Jay was just plain confused.

But one thing they all knew.

War was coming and blood would be spilt.

The question was, whose?

Twenty-One

'Thought you said you worked in a bookshop?' Miles asked, breaking the silence.

'I do,' came the simple reply.

'Who are you, Pandora?' He asked himself more than anyone else.

'She owns the bookshop,' giggled Pixie interrupting, earning a glare from Pandora. Pixie turned back around, head down like a scolded child.

Miles grumbled, rubbing his temples. 'So, a bookshop owner by day and gangster by night, sounds like a badly written book.'

'The bookshop was my fault,' admitted Pixie, turning to face Miles. 'I panicked when you asked what she did and I promised I wouldn't tell anyone, so I said she worked in a bookshop.'

'So, you bought a bookshop? A bit extreme don't you think?' asked Miles chuckling, still trying to add everything up.

'Technically Frankie went and bought the bookshop, which she thought was hilarious. When you think about it, it is a little bit funny,' Pixie continued rambling.

'Pixie, you're nervous. Breathe,' barked Pandora from the back seat.

'Why all the smoke and mirrors Pandora?' Miles asked, turning his head towards her.

'You have your secrets, Mr Miles, I have mine,' was all she would offer.

'You seem to know more about me than I know about you…' he probed.

'I prefer action over words. You'll see for yourself soon enough. We're nearly there.'

Pandora nodded at the road ahead as the outline of *Limbo* came into view. Miles bit back his next question, there was no point pressing for answers... yet.

They pulled up behind the other cars. Getting out, Miles noticed Lenny and Sparky following Frankie's directions and helping the girls into the club. As they approached the club, the doors swung open.

'Lila,' Pandora shouted, 'is Felix ready?'

'Yes, Boss, Doc is all set up,' she replied. 'Looks like you've had a peaceful night.'

'You know me Lila, always going for the easy route,' Pandora groaned.

Lila, Lila, Miles knew that name somewhere. His eyes connected with hers realising who she was.

'Boss,' Lila snapped, 'What the fuck is he doing here?'

'Don't worry Lila, you're safe. He's with us... for now,' Pandora tried to reassure her.

'Boss, I trust you with my life. You know that, but he's Miles fucking Wyatt. He belongs to Joey,' she argued, getting twitchy. Miles's face dropped to a stony glare.

'Not anymore. Joey took his sister, he needs us,' Pandora stated.

Miles cleared his throat. 'Erm, I am right here you know.'

Lila glared at him before racing over to check in with Frankie.

'You do know who she is don't you?' Miles asked Pandora.

'Yes.'

'She's Joey's girl. She belongs to him. He's been hunting high and low for her since someone shot up his boys and... It was you.'

'It was me.'

Pandora stepped towards him looking up at him.

'But let me clarify for you Mr Wyatt,' her tone was deadly, 'Lila belongs to fucking nobody. Do you get me?'

She didn't bother waiting for a reply before storming inside the club, the rage radiating off her. He followed, keeping his distance, he didn't know whether to feel worried or in awe. He was slightly annoyed they were back to 'Mr Wyatt' though. As they entered the empty club, Miles followed the group as they headed out back, along the corridors and down a level.

Pandora took charge effortlessly.

'Felix get the girls checked over and settled,' she nodded to a slender elderly man who kept pushing his oversized black glasses up his nose. He grabbed his stethoscope from his bag, getting to work with a smile.

'Nora,' Pandora beckoned a young girl over, the one Miles had seen at the bookshop.

'Yes, Boss,' she piped up eagerly.

'Help Felix. Did you grab the teddy bear?' Nora nodded. 'It's for the little one over there, Izzy, she's your responsibility. You know what to do?' Nora nodded and headed off.

'Nate, where's our new friend?'

The tall, tanned man grinned. 'He's next door in the VIP suite Boss. Didn't want him upsetting our guests,' he said politely, nodding to the girls.

'Well, it would be rude not to make him feel welcome, wouldn't it?' Pandora smirked.

That smirk. Miles got an uneasy twinge; he had a feeling there was so much he had underestimated in his dear Pandora. She turned to him with a hungry look in her eyes. 'Mr Wyatt, would you like to join me?' He realised the look wasn't for him but for her guest.

'Sparky, Lenny,' Miles said, grabbing their attention, 'stay here and help.' They nodded. 'Jay, you're with me.' Jay turned to follow.

A short walk further down the corridor they reached a room guarded by Seb. The mountain looked at Miles and Jay.

'Don't worry Seb, they're with me,' Pandora said.

'Okay, Boss,' he replied softly, stepping back to let them pass.

Miles looked at the mountain, that familiar look he'd seen in the eyes of everyone here when they looked at her.

Respect.

Even his own men were bloody well in awe of her, of course they were. He mentally slapped himself. But respect and fear were too different things. Respect couldn't replace fear. Not in this world.

Pixie was perched on a nearby table, chatting with Wayne as the three of them entered. Frankie was in the middle of the room, securing their guest. Her grin was dark.

'Hey Boss,' Frankie greeted Pandora cheerfully. 'Me and my new friend Steve here were just getting to know each other, weren't we Steve?'

71

'Is his name actually Steve?' Pandora asked, an eyebrow raised.

'I'll be fucked if I know, he hasn't talked yet. But I definitely think he looks like a Steve?' She slapped his leg, releasing a scream from him. 'Oh sorry mate, that looks sore, you might want to see someone about that. Looks like someone shot you,' Frankie winked at Pixie. 'Pixie, I thought you didn't like guns,' she teased.

'I don't,' Pixie said defensively, hands up. 'But a girl's gotta do what a girl's gotta do!'

Miles studied Pixie as her legs swung off the edge of the metal table. He could still see that sweet hostess that worked for him, but there was something else there that he hadn't noticed before, something strong and independent.

Pixie hopped off the table playfully. 'I'm gonna go help Lila if you don't need me here, I'm not a fan of the next bit.' She waved her hand towards Frankie who had an arm wrapped around her new friend.

'Don't worry Pixie, you done good!' Frankie praised as Pixie blushed, nodding to Miles and Jay as she left.

Pandora who had been quiet up until now cleared her throat.

'Frankie, I'm not trying to spoil your fun but get the fuck out of my way. I've not got the time for you to play tonight.'

Frankie's shoulders dropped. 'Yes Boss.'

Pandora slid her coat off, passing it to Wayne. Her eyes locked on her prey.

Tonight had not gone to plan. She wanted answers and she wanted them now.

Approaching with a sway of her hips, she bent over, one hand stroking the man's hair as he tried to breathe through the pain.

'Sshh, sweetie, relax. I just need some information and then this can all be over,' she reassured him, but he shook his head. 'Now that's just not going to work for me I'm afraid,' she tutted.

Pulling his head back by his hair she let her hand trail down his face, teasing down his torso and onto his leg. Using her index finger, she circled softly around the bullet wound. Without warning she shoved her delicately manicured nail into the bullet hole, releasing a gut-wrenching scream of pain.

There was no smile, no disgust, no fear or pleasure. Just a blank unreadable face. Miles and Jay looked on as she got to work.

Twenty-Two

Frankie's new friend, Not-Steve, was tougher than he looked, or just dumb. Pandora was tempted just to give him to Frankie, but she liked to play with her toys and tonight wasn't about pleasure.

Miles and Jay just stood back and watched. This wasn't their turf and these weren't their people. Part of Miles wanted to see what Pandora was really made of. Jay was still too busy with his eyes glued to Frankie who was jumping at the bit to continue. But Miles was only interested in watching Pandora. He hadn't expected her to be so brutal. He hadn't expected her to get her hands dirty. He hadn't expected her to be so fascinating to watch in action.

Everyone feared something, but tonight you could have been mistaken for thinking she was fearless. There wasn't one moment of falter or weakness with her and the fact she was a woman just made her all that more powerful.

These men who obeyed her every word could easily rip most other men into pieces, yet they were devoted to her. And these women who followed her too, they had a confidence and strength that he knew she had something to do with. How did she cement their loyalty? Was it money? Intimidation? Sex? She was a mystery to be unravelled and Miles had decided he was the one that was going to do it.

'Ciara is his new replacement for Lila,' Not-Steve screamed, as Pandora used the potato peeler across his nipple, ripping it off slowly. 'You'll never get the bitch back. You're all fucked.'

The blood gushed out and Pandora turned to the tub next to her, grabbing a handful of cornflour and packing it into the wound before picking up a small knife. Miles raised an eyebrow.

'Cornflour cauterizes the wound, stopping the bleeding. We can't have our friend saying goodbye yet.'

'So he is using Ciara to replace Lila,' Miles interrupted. 'We could trade...'

Before he could finish his sentence, Pandora spun around from Not-Steve, the knife now positioned between Miles's legs.

'I suggest you don't finish that thought,' she warned. 'Nobody is trading one of my girls.'

He noticed the emphasis on *her* girls.

'I told you I'll get her back and I will, but I'm not sacrificing one girl for another. That's not how I work.'

She knew he was desperate, but she was not about to hand Lila over to the devil. Not that it would have gained Ciara's freedom anyway.

'He won't let her go, Miles,' Pandora said softly. 'She is your weakness, and he wants to control you.'

'So what are we going to do?' Miles said almost pleading. He'd never felt so helpless.

'We're going to take her back.' she said, her face darkening as she removed the knife from its delicate position, raising it to her face before licking it slowly. She turned her back to him ramming the knife through Not-Steve's crotch without hesitation. Jay and Miles both winced, their hands reaching to their own instinctively.

Not-Steve was now gasping, unable to form words as Frankie approached, a bottle of vodka in hand. She ripped his head back forcing his mouth open and poured the vodka down his neck, not giving him the chance to swallow as he spluttered and choked.

'What a waste Frankie, that was good vodka,' Pandora grumbled. Frankie shrugged. Taking a gulp for herself with a grin, she offered the bottle to Jay and Miles. They shook their heads.

Pandora rounded back on Not-Steve. 'Nearly there, sweetie, nearly there. I just need one more answer and we're all done,' she purred.

Miles went to interrupt – he had more than one question – but Pandora raised her hand, silencing him. His mouth dropped. Nobody shushed him. He was Miles fucking Wyatt. He knew he was outnumbered here but he wasn't about to be walked over by anyone, not even her.

She comforted the bleeding man, whispering into his ears. He was starting to slip into shock. She leaned in, closely listening as he whispered exactly what she needed. What she'd been looking for all along.

She stood up, rubbing her hands together as Wayne approached her with a wet cloth. She began cleaning the blood and snot off her hands. Looking down at her shoes she grumbled, noticing a mark and rolling her eyes.

'Well?' Miles snapped impatiently.

'Well, what?' she snapped back.

'What did he say?'

'He told me where Ciara is.'

'What are we waiting for then?' Miles barked.

'Mr Wyatt, you are in my club. Calm the fuck down and show some respect,' she spat back.

'Pixie promised me if I saved your ass you would help get Ciara. It's now time to pay up your end of the bargain.'

'One, I didn't need you playing knight,' she lied, 'two I will get Ciara, not because you demand it though. I will not, however, run into this like a man. I intend to live.'

As she walked out of the room she turned to Frankie. 'He's all yours, but don't take too long. We have shit to do.' Frankie nodded at her present, watching as Pandora, Miles and Jay left the room, shutting the door as the screams erupted.

'Seb, arrange clean up when she's done,' Pandora said to her mountain, patting him gently on the chest as they left.

'Yes, Boss,' he said cheerily, as if someone had asked him to go flower picking.

Twenty-Three

Felix and most of the girls had gone when Pandora returned. Only four remained; the four that had decided to stand their ground at the warehouse.

'These four wanted to stay,' Lila confirmed.

Pandora never asked any of them to stay, this wasn't about building an army. But some of the girls were so scarred by what they had seen and been through that they needed purpose. One only Pandora could give to them.

'Has Nora gone with Izzy and the younger ones?' Pandora asked scanning the room.

'Yes,' Lila replied, 'I think Izzy was quite upset though, so Nora was going to take her back to the bookshop for now after the others were settled. Nate went with them.'

Pandora nodded in approval. 'Lila, do you want to take these four with you? Get them cleaned up and we'll work out a plan for them.' Lila nodded. One of the girls stormed up to Pandora, wrapping her arms around her. No words, just an embrace. Pandora gently patted her back, pulling away from her as she assessed the girl.

'What's your name?'

'I don't remember,' she admitted. Pandora looked her up and down, the girl was eighteen if that but the steely grey eyes that looked back at her gave her a reflection of herself.

'How about Storm? Because that's what you're going to be causing when I'm done with you, girl,' Pandora winked.

The girl nodded back, wiping her eyes, that resolve setting in. Lila beckoned the girls, sending one last glare to Miles before she left, leaving just Miles's boys, Pixie and Pandora in the room.

'Pixie, grab me a change of clothes please,' Pandora asked wearily once the girls had gone. Pixie grabbed a dress and shoes from the cupboard behind her, handing them to Pandora. Stepping out of her stained shoes, Pandora reached behind her to unzip her dress, her hand met a larger one. Wordlessly, Miles slowly pulled down the zip. He stood, chest against her back, pausing for a moment before stepping back to allow her to step out of the dress. Pandora stepped into the fresh black dress, pulling it up over her black lingerie and over her arms. Once again, she felt the sturdy set of hands behind her. She pulled her hair to the side allowing him to zip her back up before stepping back into the fresh heels.

She noticed every set of eyes in the room had watched the exchange silently.

Walking round to her desk she sat, feeling fresher without the blood splatter. Pixie removed the old clothes, shoving them in the cupboard to be cleaned later.

Pandora gestured for her guests to sit. They all took perches around the room except Pixie who stood warily between the two sides.

Miles glanced at Pixie, whose eyes hit the floor.

'I'm sorry Mr Wyatt,' she stammered, clearly torn.

'You've got nothing to be sorry for Pixie,' Pandora chimed in. 'You never betrayed him, you earned him good money. You don't belong to anyone. Remember that.'

'Says the woman who's had her working for me, spying on me,' Miles growled, his fists clenched on his lap.

'Oh, stop being a baby, Mr Wyatt. Pixie here wasn't stealing secrets or trying to bump you off, she was just one of many pairs of eyes in the grand plan. She actually really likes working for you,' Pandora said bluntly as Pixie continued to blush.

'And what is this grand plan?' Miles probed.

'That is none of your concern,' Pandora deflected. 'All you need to know is our goals align and I can help you get back Ciara.'

'Has this got anything to do with all Joey's girls that keep going missing? Are you stealing them and selling them on yourself?' he snarled accusingly.

He didn't even see the knife appear until it landed in the sofa between his legs. The rage from her was electrifying.

'They were not Joey's girls, Mr Wyatt,' Pandora spat. 'They are nobody's fucking girls. And what I do with them is none of your fucking business. Do we understand? Do you want my help or not? The fucking door is there if you don't.'

She knew she'd have to kill him if he left then, and all of his men, which would upset Pixie. But he knew too much.

Miles stared intently between her and the knife. Pulling it from the sofa, he stood and placed it gently on the desk. He'd hit a nerve.

'So, how are we going to get Ciara back then?' he asked as he sat back down.

'We're going to give Joey exactly what he wants.'

'And what is that?'

'You'll find out,' she grimaced.

Twenty-Four

Pandora had lied to Miles; she hadn't got a fucking clue where Joey was keeping his sister. But she knew exactly how to find out and she wasn't looking forward to it. She hadn't told anyone what the plan was yet, she knew they would try and stop her but this was the only way and Miles had helped save the girls and her people, so the debt had to be paid.

She'd sent Miles and his boys on their way with a promise of a plan in the next few days, so as to not arouse any suspicion. Joey didn't know Miles had intervened, as nobody had gotten out alive and the warehouse blowing up would take suspicion off Miles because nobody would be stupid enough to blow up their own warehouse, would they?

Pixie had gone with them, something Pandora could see Miles wasn't happy about but she was the easiest way to get messages between them without attracting any attention. Pandora knew Pixie was really upset about Miles thinking she'd betrayed him, especially when she'd enjoyed working for him so much. Hopefully, the damage there could be repaired with time.

She picked up her phone and dialled. 'Lila, we need to chat. Come down to the club as soon as you can today.'

She would need Lila's help for any of this to work but she knew Lila didn't trust Miles.

This wasn't about fucking Miles though. This was about Ciara and whatever other poor girls that bastard Joey was keeping locked up like animals. The mission was still the same. Only the plan had changed.

Pandora had checked in with Nora; Izzy had already got George wrapped round her little finger and Nora was thoroughly enjoying playing big sister for the moment. It obviously wasn't a permanent solution, but it would work for now.

***

Miles had returned to Temptation with Jay and Pixie in tow.

'Who the fuck does she think she is barking orders at me?' Miles shouted, slamming his fist down onto the desk.

'And you!' he roared, pointing at Pixie as she jumped, 'you've been in on this the whole time.'

'I'm sorry Mr Wyatt, I promise I haven't betrayed you,' Pixie sniffed. 'I owe Pandora a lot and everything she's doing is important.'

'But you won't tell me what that is,' he snapped.

Her eyes wouldn't meet his as she bit her lip.

Jay piped up, 'Boss, you're upsetting her.'

'Are you taking her fucking side over mine?' Miles growled quietly.

'No, Boss,' Jay defended, hands up, 'but this is Pixie we are talking about. She's only trying to help. She fucking shot people defending us last night. Cut her some slack is all I'm saying.'

Miles didn't want her at the club at the moment, she was a liability and that was dangerous. But he agreed everything needed to look normal and his sacking his favourite hostess would attract attention. He had to admit he had been quite impressed when he saw her in action. It was like a switch had been flicked, another side of his sweet Pixie, who obviously knew how to look after herself but wasn't arrogant or cocky.

He had gone from being fascinated with Pandora, to wanting to snap her neck. How could one woman cause so much conflict?

'Pixie,' he said not even looking up at her, 'shouldn't you be getting on with some work then if you're staying?'

'Yes sir,' she perked up, dashing away.

'Do you think she would betray us?' Miles asked Jay.

'No, Boss, I don't think she would,' he paused. 'But I don't think she'd betray Pandora either. Whatever Pandora has done for her lot, it's left them all willing to die for her. You saw that yourself.'

Miles pondered on this. Lila's presence alone had gotten him asking himself what Pandora had become mixed up in. She was obviously the one stealing the shipments. But was she the source of the conflict between the gangs too? Whatever game she was playing it was a dangerous one, but she didn't seem to mind the risk of getting burned.

Watching her torture Joey's guy, she hadn't seemed to be enjoying it in the same way as Frankie but there was no disgust, no remorse nor upset at what she was doing. It was cold and calculated. He knew how *he'd* become that way but how did a young woman become a cold ruthless killer? Something happened to make her. He needed to know what he was getting involved with.

'We need to know more about Pandora. See what we missed. There must be something.'

'Yes, Boss,' said Jay, saluting before running out of the office.

There were so many mysteries with this woman and every time he thought the rabbit hole couldn't go deeper, it did. But she said she had a plan and it was his only hope of getting Ciara back in one piece. Joey wouldn't kill her while he needed Miles but there were so many things worse than death.

Twenty-Five

'Boss, no!'

'Frankie, it's not up for debate,' Pandora snapped.

'It's fucking suicide,' Frankie tried to reason.

'Only if I die.'

Pandora knew the risks she was taking, she knew she was more than likely screwed and she knew it was the only way.

Joey had almost cornered them all in the warehouse, she couldn't keep on with the original plan; it wasn't feasible anymore. But the new plan was...

'The new plan is fucking stupid,' Frankie sighed, pouring herself a drink.

'Don't you think it's a bit early for that?' Pandora nodded to the glass.

'You're driving me to it, Boss,' she replied, passing Pandora a matching glass.

'If you can't beat them, join them.' Pandora took the glass, gulping the amber liquid down in one go, the burning sensation flushing down her throat as she swallowed.

'He's not going to agree to this, you know,' said Frankie nursing her glass.

'He will if he wants to see his sister again,' Pandora knew he would agree. He only had one goal and she could understand. It hurt, but she understood.

'Everything else in place?' Pandora changed the subject.

'Yes, Boss, down to the last detail.'

'Okay, call him. No point putting it off.'

As Pandora entered the bookshop, a wave of apprehension flooded over her. Her mind logically knew what had to happen but her body, still scarred with the horrors of her past, screamed at her to run, to hide. It wasn't a choice she could oblige.

Mr Talbot had a cup of hot chocolate waiting for her as she sat at the counter next to him.

'The girls gone out?' Pandora asked as she nursed the mug in her hands.

'Yes. Frankie suggested Nora take the little one out for the day, I think they've gone to the park,' he replied softly.

They sat in a comfortable silence. In another life, another world, she could have been quite content here in the bookshop, surrounded by a thousand lives hidden in the pages.

She glanced at her watch again before meeting the old man's eyes.

'You sure you don't want me to stay?' he asked.

'No, you go run your errands, I'm perfectly capable of watching the shop for half an hour. What's the worst that could happen?' she half chuckled.

He looked at her once more, gently placing a hand on her shoulder before grabbing his coat to head out. She took a sip from her cup, making the most of the silence as the door clicked behind her.

***

Taking a book out from under the counter she opened its pages.

"Anything one man can imagine; other men can make real."

'Around the World in 80 Days.' The low voice came from the doorway.

Pandora looked up at the visitor.

'Yes, have you read it, Mr Wyatt?' she asked with a half-smile.

'No, can't say I have, books aren't really my thing.'

He smirked, his eyes locked on her as he edged closer. It was a lie and she knew it. It was one of his favourite books, he knew the lines by memory.

Still moving closer cautiously, he heard the door behind him. He knew they couldn't follow simple instructions but he also knew there was a high probability of a gun pointing in his direction under that counter.

He couldn't underestimate her.

'To what do I owe the pleasure, Mr Wyatt?' she smiled sweetly at him, putting him on edge with her honey tones.

'I think you know exactly why we're here,' his low tone growled back.

He knew Joey's boys were behind him, itching for some action but he couldn't mess this up.

'Well, this is a bookshop, Mr Miles, so one would assume you'd be here for a book. Not sure if we've got anything interesting for your… friends though. We don't stock many picture books,' she smirked, she couldn't help that tongue of hers.

'Lucky for you then,' he replied stepping closer, 'books are the last thing we're wanting today.'

Miles saw it in her eyes, she was about to react. He braced himself ready for shots but she darted instead. He cursed mentally, jumping the counter to grab her, his left hand round her throat and his gun to her temple.

He could feel the pounding of her pulse, her heavy breathing as she calculated ways to escape his grasp, but he knew he had her. He wasn't letting her go. Ciara needed him.

Pandora had made her choices and so had he.

'Mr Siegel would like a word with you.'

He could see Joey's boys had questions; he could see they wanted to play with her. He wasn't going to let them near her. He needed her delivered to Joey in one piece. A job he was going to do personally.

Lenny was waiting by the car, a flash of guilt in his face as he watched Miles walk Pandora towards him. Miles glared at him, sending his gaze anywhere but the pair of them as he shoved Pandora into the backseat.

Lenny got into the driver's seat, pulling his belt on. The engine growled into life as he looked into the rear-view mirror at Miles.

'Lenny, you know where to go. Stop stalling,' he snapped.

Lenny gave Pandora an apologetic glance and she smiled back forgivingly; she knew the choice wasn't his. It wasn't really Miles's choice either. It was her own choices that had brought her to this point.

Miles didn't release her from his grip, but he did move his hand from her throat to her arm. The gun stayed poised though. He knew she wasn't worth underestimating. She gave him a small knowing smirk but stayed silent.

'If there had been another way...' he trailed off.

She shrugged, rolling her eyes.

'I hope you understand, this isn't personal Pan,' he reasoned.

'You trying to convince me or yourself?' she spat.

He huffed, giving up. There was no reasoning with her. He couldn't blame her though. Returning to silence, he clenched his jaw. He was doing the right thing. It would all be over soon and Ciara would be safe, then he could forget he'd ever met Pandora.

But would he ever be able to forget?

Twenty-Six

The drive was over much quicker than Pandora had hoped. As the car pulled up, Lenny took one final glance, meeting Pandora's eyes in the rear-view mirror before she was yanked out of the car by Miles.

Pandora froze as they got out of the car. Her feet planted. Panic took over. She prayed she'd never have to return here but at least this would be the last time; one way or another.

The force she was dragged with gripped tightly into her bicep, her feet trailing as she tried desperately to hold her ground.

Even his glare wasn't enough to force her to move freely, she knew what was ahead was much worse than anything he could do to her right now. But unwillingly she drew closer to the building anyway, his unrelenting grip moving her towards the opening door.

Joey's boys followed closely; vultures ready to follow the blood trail.

The dimly lit room revealed a small army of thugs and brutes dotted about, but her focus was pulled to the two figures in the middle of the room. The quivering blood and the smirk of the devil.

'Miles, my dear boy, what present have you brought me today?' His voice dripped with venom as he stroked Ciara's hair softly.

'Joey, I'm here for my sister,' Miles hissed through clenched teeth.

'But we're just getting to know each other,' Joey grinned, grabbing Ciara's hair and sniffing it.

Miles pulled himself back, stopping mid-step.

'I have something you want. I'm willing to trade.'

'You have nothing, boy. Who is this whore you've brought me?' he chuckled at Pandora. 'I'm not ready to downgrade, I've barely got to know your sister yet.'

Joey stroked Ciara's face as she sobbed, her face flooded with tears.

'This whore is more valuable than you think Joey,' Miles teased.

Pandora gritted her teeth, eyes scanning the room. Exits, windows, weapons, there had to be an answer.

'Stop fucking about with me boy, screw your riddles and tell me before I lose my cool and start showing you just how impatient I can be.' Joey yanked Ciara's hair back, putting his gun up to her head.

'I'm not fucking you about. You wanted me to find out who had been fucking with you. This is it.'

He shoved Pandora to her knees in front of Joey. Pandora's body shivered, she kept her face down, focussing on her breathing.

'You want me to believe this dirty little whore is the one who's responsible for everything?'

Miles's face told Joey he wasn't fucking about.

'You're serious?'

Miles nodded.

'The men you lost at the docks the other night?' he said and Joey nodded for him to continue. 'I did some digging. It was her.'

'And she took Lila…'

Pandora's head snapped up. She launched at Miles landing her fist straight in his nose before he could stop her. The blood pissed out down his freshly ironed shirt.

He glanced at Pandora who was now pinned by two of Joey's men who had grabbed her, grinning at the opportunity of getting their hands on her. The hatred in her eyes was clear, she would never forgive him. He doubted she'd live long enough to be able to dwell on it.

'So we have a trade?' Miles pushed, wanting to grab Ciara and get out of there.

Joey released his grip on Ciara's hair, approaching the seething Pandora as she hissed and struggled on the floor. Leaning down, he reached out to pull her fiery hair out of her face, to get a look at the accused.

Pandora was pinned; no matter how much she struggled they gripped tighter, laughing. As Joey's hand reached her face, she snapped, biting down as hard as she could.

'FUCKING BITCH!!!' Joey screamed trying to pull his hand back but her teeth clamped down harder, blood filling her mouth.

A fist connected with her jaw, making her release his mangled bloody hand.

One of his men handed him a cloth to wrap around the dripping wound. Using his intact hand he wrenched her head up by her hair. She grinned at him, his blood dripping from her mouth.

That face, those eyes. They looked so familiar.

'Pandora...' he whispered, remembering.

'You know her?' Miles interrupted.

Joey stood speechless as Pandora continued to snarl at him.

'Joey,' Miles snapped, 'do we have a deal?'

'Yes,' waved Joey absently, 'have the bitch. You've just given me something much more valuable.'

Ciara was released, throwing herself into her brother's arms. He wanted to know what was going on, but not enough to risk keeping Ciara there any longer. Draping his jacket around, her he began to lead her out.

'Miles,' she whispered, 'we can't just leave Pan there. She's my friend.'

'And she was the price of your freedom, Ciara,' sighed Miles not allowing himself to glance back as he guided her out.

Joey, oblivious to the exiting pair, kept his focus on the ghost before him. Where had all that fire come from? No matter, he'd broken her once before and he'd do it again.

'Welcome home my dear,' he whispered as Pandora's eyes flickered between fear and hatred. 'It's good to have you back.'

Twenty-Seven

As the fog began to lift, Pandora groaned, holding her head. Sliding herself up on the soft satin sheets, she pulled herself into a sitting position. The room was still spinning.

'What the fuck?' she mumbled.

She wasn't in a cell or a basement as far as she could tell, but she had no clue what they'd used to knock her out. Quickly rubbing her hands over her arms and neck she checked for needle marks and let out a sigh of relief when she found none.

But it was short-lived as the door opened and a familiar face entered.

'Long time no see, Pan. We've missed you,' he teased with a wink.

'I can't say the feeling's mutual Dom,' Pandora groaned at the muscular form that approached closer.

'Boss wants you to join him for dinner. He's sent you a gift.' Dom dropped a box down onto the bed next to Pandora.

'Get ready,' he said as he left the room with a click.

Resisting the urge to throw the box at the locked door, Pandora opened it knowing what was most likely inside. Pulling the dress out, she ran her hands over the emerald silk, underneath it was a pair of silver-heeled shoes and of course a silver necklace with an emerald teardrop. He always liked his toys to look good, to show off, and he always loved her in green.

She fucking hated green.

There was no way out of the room. Resisting would lead to a bullet and most likely a painful one, so she did the only thing she could; she began to get ready. Time to play the game, only this time she was a lot wiser.

She smoothed down the dress as she stepped into the heels and knocked on the door.

'Dom, I know you're out there.'

There was a click and a dark head of hair popped round the door.

'You ready?'

'Nearly,' she sighed. 'Can you do my zip please?'

He stood behind her, gently holding the fabric of the dress and pulled the zip up slowly against the soft skin of her back.

'You know how this goes Pan,' he warned. 'Don't push his buttons and this may go smoothly.'

Pandora turned to him.

'Dom, I don't know what you mean…'

'Pan, I'm warning you. For your own good.'

'Let's just get this over with.'

Pandora silently followed Dom down the halls, noting the doors and windows. She remembered each one, as the memories came flooding back.

As they entered the dining room, he was already sitting at the table. Dom pulled out a chair for her next to him before nodding and leaving the room.

Her eyes met his, the cold dark pools of the devil himself. Pandora focussed on her breathing as he reached towards her, taking her hand softly in his.

'I thought I'd lost you,' he smiled, 'but now I have you back by my side.' His grin widened. 'I knew from the very first moment I found you at that auction that you were meant to be mine, Pandora.'

Food was brought out. She looked at it blankly. She couldn't eat.

'Eat,' it wasn't a request.

Pandora slowly picked up the fork with her free hand, taking a small bite of the pasta as he continued to talk, one hand still possessively over hers. She couldn't hear what he was saying, his words merging into one as she tried to ignore the flood of memories. He was being a gentleman for now but they both knew Joey Siegel was anything but a gentleman.

'Pandora,' he called again, her eyes rising from the plate.

'I asked you a question,' his hand squeezed slightly harder. 'Did you miss me?'

Pandora gulped. She knew what she was supposed to say. She knew what she had said so many times all those years ago. She knew what would happen if she didn't. Softly she placed her fork down, removing the temptation to do what she really wanted with it.

'Joey,' she paused. 'Do you want me to say what you want to hear, or the actual truth?'

Her head tilted slightly, waiting. His gaze darkened; the smile dropped as she continued.

'Do you want me to tell you how grateful I am to be back here and how I've missed being your toy, or would you like me to tell you how I am currently resisting the urge to take this fork and ram it through your eye socket?' She raised an eyebrow and allowed a small smirk she knew she would pay for.

He released her hand, both of his now clenched. Pandora waited for the explosion. It didn't come. That unnerved her even more.

Standing, he extended a hand, Pandora complied.

'Dance with me, Pan, just like old times; it's been too many years.'

Placing his hands on her hips, he pulled her closer while swaying to the soft music. If it had been anywhere else, with anyone else, it could have been almost romantic. But this wasn't about romance, this was about control.

Pandora knew she could injure him, most likely even kill him. But there was no way she was taking out all his men too, not by herself. The temptation was there, to try and at least go out with a blaze of glory, but there would always be another Joey ready to take his place.

Stepping back, Joey took her hand softly, leading her down the corridors. A hauntingly familiar walk. Her feet got heavier but Joey led her on.

The door. That door. His door.

Pandora's body began to shake. If Joey noticed he never let on as he opened the door, leading her into his bedroom. Standing behind her, he whispered into her ear.

'I'm not letting you out of my sight this time. Where I go, you go.'

He slowly pulled the zip down on her dress, loosening it from her body.

'There's some nightwear on the bed for you,' he gestured.

Still holding her dress in place at the front she scooped up the night clothes, darting for the adjoining bathroom.

'I don't remember you being so shy,' Joey chuckled from the bedroom.

Pandora gripped onto the side of the sink, desperately trying to steady her breathing. She was trapped but she didn't know if she could do what it would take to survive. Not again.

Quickly changing, she headed back out to the bedroom, dress and shoes in hand; no point delaying the inevitable. She handed him back the clothes.

'No need, they are yours,' he smiled sweetly. She almost had to remind herself of the monster she was facing. Taking the necklace off, she placed it on the side with the clothes, plonking the shoes on the floor.

He approached the bed, getting under the covers and gesturing for her to do the same. Pulling her close, he wrapped his arms around her, holding her to his chest so she couldn't wriggle away. Her body tensed, waiting, but he simply held her silently.

She lay there wide awake, trapped in his grip, waiting for him to wake up and want more. He always wanted more. The thought made bile rise up in her throat threatening to spew. This was just the calm before the storm and she knew it was going to hit her like a fucking tornado.

Twenty-Eight

'There's got to be something we can do Frankie!' Lila snapped.

'Orders are orders Lila,' Frankie sighed running her hands through her hair.

'I can't go back there,' Pixie butted in, 'not after what he's done.'

'But you have to Pixie,' Frankie pleaded. 'Give him the silent treatment, put laxatives in his drink for all I fucking care but you need to go back. Make him think you have no choice, that you need the job now that she's…' She couldn't finish the sentence.

'But won't he wonder why I just haven't come back to you?'

'Let him wonder. Just keep your head down, we need intel now more than ever.'

'And what are we going to do about her?' Lila butted in.

'Nothing, for now. We act as if everything is normal. Business goes on. Those were her orders if anything were to happen.' Frankie couldn't even bring herself to use her name.

'Lila, make sure to keep checking in on the bookshop.' Lila nodded to Frankie, taking her leave.

'Pixie, you don't want to be late for work, just try not to do anything stupid,' Frankie begged. 'Last thing we need is war at the moment, so be smart, think with your head. Remember it's what keeps us ahead of those fuckers.'

'But what's the point of any of this without her?' Pixie sniffed, trying to hold her composure.

'This is for her. Don't forget that, or what we owe her.'

The message was clear.

As Pixie left, Frankie felt like her head was going to explode. She knew what she was supposed to do but none of this felt right.

Miles sat at his desk, staring blankly at the books. Ciara was safe, settled and protected, so why couldn't he just focus?

He knew exactly why, but he'd had no choice and she knew that. Family came first. She was probably already dead. His stomach turned at the thought. It was a new experience. Death didn't bother him, but the possibility of hers certainly seemed to.

The door opened and his jaw dropped.

'Have you got the bookings list for tonight, Mr Wyatt?'

She looked pissed off, he couldn't blame her. He glanced her up and down, no obvious sign of a gun. That didn't mean there wasn't one.

'What are you doing here, Pixie?'

'I work here,' she raised an eyebrow, arms now crossed, 'unless you're firing me?'

Keeping her would mean watching his back constantly. But something wouldn't let him fire her.

'No, here you go,' he handed her the book. 'Let me know if you need anything further.'

She took the book and left without replying, barging past Jay as she exited.

'Did you fire her?' asked Jay.

'Probably should, but I haven't,' Miles sighed. 'Might sleep with one eye open though, now I know what she's capable of.'

'Can you blame her for being pissed off?'

'Don't start with me. You know I had no choice.'

'I'm not judging, Boss, just stating facts,' Jay replied, hands up.

'I know. Ciara isn't talking to me either,' he sighed. She had been giving him the silent treatment ever since she found out the cost of her freedom.

'She'll come round Boss. She's gotta know you did what you had to. Family first and always.'

'She may understand, but it doesn't mean she'll forgive me.'

'Have you heard from Joey?'

'Only a message.'

'What did it say?' Jay looked confused.

'It was an invite to a party.'

'You gonna go, Boss?'

'Don't think I have a choice. It does say to bring a plus one, though.'

'You want me to come with you, Boss?'

'Don't think that's the type of plus one it meant Jay and I don't think you'd pull off a dress and heels,' Miles chuckled.

'I'd suggest Pixie but…'

'Suggest me for what?' Pixie asked as she re-entered the room.

'Nothing,' Miles replied.

'Didn't seem like nothing, sir,' she gritted out the word sir.

Miles sighed. 'Joey is holding a party—'

'I'd love to accompany you,' she interrupted. 'I've got the perfect outfit.'

'You're not coming,' Miles grumbled.

'Why?' she asked sweetly.

'You know exactly why.'

'Don't you trust me, Mr Wyatt?'

'No, I don't to be honest Pixie.'

'Ouch, I'm offended, Mr Wyatt. If you change your mind, I'll happily accompany you and I promise to be on my best behaviour,' she winked. 'After all, you never know when you might need a date that's handy in unpredictable situations.'

She turned to leave.

'Okay, you can come. But if you screw me over Pixie, I'll put a bullet in you myself. No matter how good you are.'

'Yes, Boss,' she saluted. 'Just let me know when and where.'

'Tomorrow night. I'll pick you up.'

Nodding, she excused herself.

'Boss,' Jay warned, 'that may have just been the stupidest thing you've ever done.'

'Yes,' he agreed, 'you're right. But if Joey does turn on me, at least I know, or I hope, Pixie hates him more than me and we both know she's more capable than any date I could take without arousing any suspicion.'

Jay nodded in agreement. Miles was dicing with his own neck, but something didn't feel right about the invite.

'Jay,' Miles continued, 'you'll stay with Ciara tomorrow night just to be safe.'

'Yes, Boss.'

Miles wasn't sure if this was going to be a party or a massacre, but he needed to be prepared.

Twenty-Nine

Pandora woke to an empty bed. She let out a breath but noticed a neatly folded pile of clothes with a note on it.

Meet me for breakfast when you wake – J

She looked at the clock, 8 a.m. She could roll over and pretend to stay asleep until someone got her but she knew it was a bad idea. Pulling herself out of bed, she got dressed. A simple blouse and trousers with plain black heels. All designer, all expensive. All to show she was his. But she wasn't his and she would never be anyone's property ever again.

Strutting down the hallway, head high shoulders back, she met his gaze as she entered the dining room. His grin sent shivers down her spine.

'You sleep well, my dear Pan?'

She ignored him, sitting down at the place set next to him.

'You still upset with me my dear?' he smirked. 'Don't worry, you'll soon get used to being back home.'

Her stomach twisted at the thought.

'However,' he continued, 'we do need to have a little chat, my dear.'

He pushed his chair back, leaning over to her, pulling her chair towards him, his legs locking hers in place. She gasped, trying to stay seated and resisting the urge to rip his throat out with her teeth as she stared at his open collar.

'I've given you time to settle back in, but I want answers, Pan. Miles tells me it was you that was disrupting my shipments?'

He gripped her jaw with his good hand, the other still bandaged from her bite.

'Well, my little fireball?'

'Yes,' she hissed, 'and I'd do it all over again.'

She waited for the impact but it didn't come, he was smirking.

'I'm impressed. But how did you manage it? Who helped you?'

Frankie, Lila, Pixie, Wayne, so many more.

'Muscle for hire, you know they don't care as long as they get paid,' she sneered.

'And where did you get that kind of money, my dear?' he probed curiously.

She stayed silent. The club, her empire, she wasn't about to hand it over to him.

'Did you sell yourself for it? Did you let people touch what's mine?' he growled, his grip tightening.

'No,' she replied honestly. 'And I'm not yours,' she whispered.

'So where did you get the money? I won't ask again,' he said calmly, the fire still clear in his eyes.

'I stole it of course.'

'From me?'

'From everywhere I had to.'

He eyed her suspiciously and she couldn't tell if he'd bought the lie. She hadn't stolen it. She'd worked from the ground up and earned every penny, but she couldn't have him tracing it back to the others. She swore she'd protect them and she would. Any way she could.

'Well, it seems you've grown a backbone, my dear. I'm quite liking the new feisty you,' he grinned, releasing his grip on her jaw. 'To celebrate having you home, I'm throwing a party.'

He didn't just throw parties, Pandora knew this, there was an agenda at play.

'I'm not in the mood for a party.'

'I thought you might say that, so I brought a little incentive,' his grin widened, the devil clear in front of her. The doors opened and Dom entered, but he wasn't alone. A small hand holding his giant one and a small head of flaming red locks bounced into the room with him, grinning.

'Who is this?' Pandora stammered, fearing the answer.

'Your daughter of course.' He held his hand out to the small girl who ran to him as he lifted her onto his knee.

'You're lying,' she hissed, the tears now flowing freely.

'Why is the pretty lady crying Daddy?'

'She's just super happy to meet you, Mia. Remember I told you we had a special visitor?'

The small girl nodded.

'Well, this is her, this is your mother.'

Jumping from Joey's lap, the small girl approached Pandora.

'Please don't cry Mommy. You're home now.' She wrapped her arms around Pandora, who instinctively did the same. Looking over the child's shoulder, she glared at the devil who was now full beam.

Checkmate.

'Mia, you go and play with Uncle Dom while Mommy and I have breakfast then I'm sure she'll want to come and play with you,' he softly spoke.

Mia tiptoed up to Pandora's cheek, kissing her before running back to Dom who wouldn't meet Pandora's gaze. As soon as the child was gone, Pandora snapped.

'I don't know what fucked up game you think this is but I'm not falling for it. And the fact you've stooped so low to taking girls that young just shows how fucked up you are.'

His hand shot out, gripping her throat and pinning her in the chair.

'My dear Pandora, I have no need to lie. She is yours; we can run a DNA test if you want. But you know just by looking at her, she is yours.'

'No. Mia died.'

'No, I took Mia away and paid off the doctor to tell you she'd died. She was a distraction. You are mine. But now it seems she serves a better use.'

Pandora's head ran through every scenario. There had been no intel, no rumours, not a peep about a child. This could all be an elaborate scam to make her compliant; easy enough to find a child with red hair.

But what if it wasn't? She had never held her daughter's cold body, she had never seen the physical proof, the grief had been too overwhelming. But even Joey wouldn't have lied about her daughter, their daughter... would he?

'What do you want?' she hissed, fists clenched as she fought back the urge to lunge at him.

'Obedience.'

Thirty

As Pixie approached the car, Miles stood with the door open.

'What a gentleman,' she muttered, getting in.

He sighed as he shut the door, walking round to get in the other side.

'Pixie, before we go anywhere…' he started.

'Yes, I know, best behaviour, no killing people and no funny business,' she sighed.

'I mean it,' he warned. 'I'm still not sure taking you is the best idea. Why do you want to come anyway?'

'It's my duty.'

'It's not part of your job role for me,' he said confused.

'I didn't say for you.'

'Explain.'

'I made a promise to her. I don't break my promises.'

'What kind of promise?'

'That was between me and her. All you need to know is I am still your faithful employee… Mr Wyatt, it's what she wanted.'

The answers did not fill him with confidence and he contemplated taking her back and making an excuse why he'd come without a date, but it was too late, they were approaching Joey's.

'You armed?'

'Always,' she smirked.

'Are they going to find it?'

'Not unless I want them to,' she winked.

Pulling up, he opened the door and offered her a hand. The mask switched on and delicate little Pixie got out the car, blushing.

'Thank you, Mr Wyatt,' she cooed, softly pecking him on the cheek.

It unnerved him how quickly she could switch but made him realise why she was so good at what she did. It was effortless.

As they approached the entrance, Miles opened his jacket ready to be searched. No weapons allowed, except Joey's of course.

'Have a good evening Mr Wyatt,' the guard nodded.

'What, don't I get a pat down?' Pixie giggled, running her hand down the guard's chest. He gulped nervously at Miles who was glaring at him.

'No Miss, I don't think Mr Wyatt would approve,' he stammered.

'Oh, ignore him, he's just a big teddy bear. Maybe later?' She blew him a kiss, walking in as the guard continued to quiver under Miles's gaze.

'Mr Wyatt, would you escort me to the bathroom?' Pixie asked as they entered the party.

He nodded, leading the way.

'Do you actually need the bathroom already?' he asked.

'No, but I wasn't going to just hand you a gun in front of everyone was I? Turn around.'

As he turned his back to her, he felt the cold metal being tucked into the back of his trousers.

'Do you have one as well?'

'That's for me to know, Mr Wyatt. A girl doesn't kiss and tell.' She reached up, giving him a kiss on the cheek as a group walked by.

'Shall we join the party, sir?'

He sighed, dreading what was coming next. One gun wasn't getting him out of here in one piece if Joey decided he was no longer worth being alive.

Putting his hand round Pixie's waist, he led her in as she smiled sweetly and glided effortlessly in her heels next to him. He was still trying to work out where she could be hiding a gun under that dress. Its black fitted form didn't leave much space to hide anything and the slit up the right leg left most of her thigh exposed.

'Ah!' came the voice Miles was dreading. 'The man of the hour...' Joey cheered.

Miles was on high alert, looking for any signs of a trap. But from the surface, it just looked like a party. A party filled with very dangerous people, but a party nonetheless.

'Mr Siegel,' Miles greeted as Joey shook his hand.

'And who is this angel you've brought with you tonight? I thought you may have brought Ciara?' he grinned, knowing just the right nerve to hit.

'No,' paused Miles, 'she had plans unfortunately so she sent her apologies. This here is Pixie, one of my hostesses at the club.'

Pixie blushed on cue as Joey took her hand, kissing it delicately.

'Well, she can host me any day,' he winked.

Pixie giggled. 'Oh Mr Siegel, you charmer. You are too sweet.'

Joey kissed her hand once more before heading towards the doors at the back of the room and clearing his throat for everyone's attention. Silence fell immediately.

'Friends,' Joey began, 'thank you for joining me tonight, on this special occasion.'

There was a murmur around the room.

'I am delighted to announce that my Pandora was finally brought safely home to me, thanks to Miles Wyatt.' Joey raised his hand towards Miles before the doors behind him opened. Miles and Pixie both quickly composed themselves as the familiar head of red hair walked into the room, a long silver strappy dress hugging her curves as she smiled confidently, settling by Joey's side.

Thirty-One

As Pandora entered the room, she scanned the crowd. Everyone in the room was loyal to Joey. Everyone except one. Maybe two.

She saw Pixie with Miles.

Not letting her gaze linger too long she settled next to Joey, looping her hands round his arm as he spoke.

'And to celebrate her return, I would also like to announce,' he continued reaching into his pocket, 'our engagement!'

The room erupted into applause and Pandora froze. The bastard. She couldn't react, not in front of this many people. Not with the threat he'd made earlier.

Mia.

Regardless of whether she was hers or not, she was an innocent child, one she knew Joey would use against her, whether he was Mia's father or not.

Smiling, Pandora watched as Joey placed the ring on her finger, feeling the weight of the shackle that now bound her to him even more. As the applause died down, he whispered in her ear, 'Good girl, now go dance and play nice with the guests and I might let you see Mia before bed.'

He was dangling her like a tasty carrot but Pandora couldn't care less at that moment, she had one aim for the night.

Nodding she headed out through the crowd, bumping into Dom.

'I thought you were watching Mia,' she snapped.

'No, he's got one of the old women from the house staff watching her.'

'Dance with me Dom,' she asked, causing him to step back.

'Why?'

'I've got to dance and play nice and if I can avoid the sleazy hands of any of those dickheads I will.'

He nodded, carefully placing his hand on her hips so they weren't too low.

'Joey's got you well trained, I see,' she sneered, leaning into him.

'I like my kneecaps,' he laughed.

'So, tell me honestly, is the kid mine?'

'He said she is, but I didn't even know she existed 'til you came back. Apparently, he's had her hid away somewhere being looked after by a nanny or some shit.'

'That doesn't prove anything,' Pandora replied.

'No, it doesn't but this isn't just about the kid, it's about keeping yourself alive. You had to know the day would come when he'd find you. How could you be so stupid to play these games?'

'Because I wasn't going to be someone's toy anymore,' Pandora sighed.

'And how's that working out for you?' he teased.

'You're a right cunt, you know that don't you?'

'You're not exactly an angel yourself.'

As the song came to an end, the pair were parted.

'Do you mind if I cut in Dom?' Miles asked.

'As long as your date won't mind?' he said looking over at Pixie who smiled sweetly at them.

'Not at all, I'm sure she wouldn't mind keeping you company,' replied Miles.

Nodding, Dom headed over to Pixie who eyed him like a piece of meat.

'Aren't you going to ask me if I even want to dance with you Mr Wyatt?' she growled quietly.

'I'm glad you're alive,' he whispered, pulling her in to dance.

'No thanks to you.'

'You know I only did what I had to for Ciara. You know that,' he hissed.

'That's not what I'm pissed off about,' she sighed.

'What?' he stepped back surprised before she pulled him back in.

'I knew you would, I'd set you up to do it, but you just had to go and mention fucking Lila!' she sneered.

Miles was confused, she didn't hate him for potentially sending her to her death. She hated him for letting Joey know she took Lila.

'If he finds Lila, I'll personally put a bullet in you myself, Mr Miles,' she said sweetly as they continued to dance round the room.

'I think you should be more concerned about yourself,' he warned.

'Don't worry about me Mr Miles, I'm right where I need to be.'

Thirty-Two

As Pandora and Miles parted, Pandora felt a hand on her shoulder.

'Since you're free I thought I'd grab the next dance,' a man she didn't recognise grinned at her, a gold tooth glinting. One of Joey's thugs.

'Maybe later, I'm just going to grab a drink,' Pandora suggested.

'No, how about now? Or I tell Joey what a disobedient little bitch you're being.'

Pandora relented, allowing him to lead in the dance, his hands on her hips.

'I can see what Joey likes about you,' he licked his lips. 'Maybe he'll think about sharing you when he gets bored.'

His hands started to wander lower.

'I don't think Joey likes to share,' whispered Pandora, 'and I'd think twice before letting those hands wander if you'd like to keep them.'

He laughed loudly, grabbing her arse. 'You think too much of yourself bitch.'

Pandora tried to pull away, but his grip was too tight and he pulled her closer.

She had warned him. He didn't listen. He also didn't notice the bullet to the back of his head.

Joey grinned, simply stepping over him to continue his previous conversation as Dom beckoned in several men to remove the leaking corpse from the floor.

'Are you okay?' a small woman said sweetly. 'I think you've got a bit of blood on you, let me help you get cleaned up.'

Pandora glanced at Joey who nodded, looking down at the 'bit of blood' that was more like an entire splatter. Joey was unhinged and his behaviour tonight just confirmed that. She followed the woman across the room.

'My names Pixie, I'm here with Mr Wyatt,' she introduced herself. 'Let's get you to the bathroom and get you all sparkly and fresh!'

Pixie took Pandora's hand, leading her to the bathroom Miles had shown her.

Once in the bathroom, Pixie checked to see it was empty before jumping on Pandora.

'Oh my God, Boss, I'm so happy you're alive!' she squealed.

'Tone down the theatrics, we haven't got time,' Pandora snapped.

'Sorry, Boss, what's the exit strategy? You want me to create a distraction?' Pixie suggested.

'No, not yet,'

'What! We need to get you out of here!' Pixie pleaded. 'You don't have that Stockholm Syndrome do you?'

'Don't be stupid, I just can't leave yet. It's complicated.' She paused. 'Miles let it slip to Joey about Lila and there's a kid. He says it's mine.'

'But it can't be!' Pixie's mouth gaped.

'I know but she's still a kid. If I run now, he'll go after Lila and the kid will be in danger. No, we play the long game here. We stick to the plan. Okay? You playing nice with Miles?'

'Yes,' Pixie grumbled.

'Is Ciara okay?' Pandora asked, concerned.

'I think so, I haven't been able to see her yet.'

'Make sure you check in on her. Make sure she's all right.'

'Do you want me to leave you my phone or my gun, Boss?' Pixie offered.

'No, it would be too dangerous if it was found. Right, we need to go back,' Pandora pointed out as she wiped the blood from her face.

Pixie pulled her into one more squeeze of a hug, before they both left the toilet.

'You're too bloody soft Pixie,' Pandora teased as they walked out.

By the time Pandora and Pixie re-entered the party the body was gone, and any sign of the previous incident had already been removed.

'Thank you for your help, Pixie, it was very kind of you,' said Pandora as they approached Miles and Joey.

Joey wrapped his arm tightly around Pandora's waist.

'My apologies about that my dear, some people just have no manners,' he chuckled.

Pixie chuckled along too, and Pandora forced an awkward smile.

'Pixie here is one of Miles's hostesses,' Joey grinned to Pandora. 'I told her she could host me any day, I'm sure I could share her with you Pandora. She's just delicious to look at, isn't she?' he licked his lips.

'Sounds delightful,' Pandora replied through gritted teeth, aware of the eyes around the room.

'Aww you're too sweet Mr Siegel,' Pixie sighed, blushing.

'Well, you two enjoy dancing,' Joey nodded to Pixie and Miles. 'I'm going to steal my fiancée away for a dance.'

Leading her away, Joey pulled her into his arms, swaying to the music. Pandora scanned the room looking at all the happy faces and wondering how many of them were a mask just like hers.

'You look deep in thought my fiancée. What are you thinking about?' he enquired.

'You don't want to know,' she warned.

'Oh, but I do.'

'So, you want to know in great detail how I daydream about gliding a blade across that thick throat of yours and slowly watching the life drain out of you?' she smiled sweetly.

'Don't worry my dear, you will come around, and you will come to me willingly,' he assured her.

So that was his plan, to break her until she offered herself willingly. He'd be waiting a long fucking time, thought Pandora.

Thirty-Three

The tension was suffocating in the car between Pixie and Miles.

'Just say it,' Miles snapped.

'What?'

'Whatever it is that you're bubbling over, Pixie,' he growled.

'Pan told me what you did!' she screamed, almost causing him to veer off the road.

'I did what I had to do to save Ciara, you know that!'

'Not that, you dimwit! You told Joey about Lila. How could you?'

'Wait so you're not mad about me handing Pandora over, but about me name-dropping Lila? Pandora said the same thing. Explain to me what the fuck is going on,' he threatened, pulling over.

'Do you have some crayons so I can draw you a picture?' she glared.

Pulling the gun from behind him, he placed it against her forehead.

'Don't test me Pixie,' he warned.

'One. The safety is still on. Two. You like this car too much to get my blood all over it. Three. You are a fucking idiot,' her smirk widened.

He lowered the gun, grumbling; she knew him too well, it was unnerving.

'We knew you would trade Pan for Ciara. We were betting on you going through with it. Pandora knew it was the only way to save Ciara for you,' she explained. 'But then you had to go and tell him about Lila, so now if Pan manages somehow to escape, he'll come after Lila and then most likely find us all. It's not like she'll leave anyway with the kid there though,' Pixie mumbled.

'Kid? What kid?'

'Some kid Joey is pretending is Pan's. What, you didn't think she'd be this obedient tonight if there wasn't a reason for it?'

Miles had thought it strange that someone as fiery and dangerous as Pandora would willingly play along with Joey.

'I've never heard about a kid before,' he muttered.

'Nobody has,' Pixie piped in. 'Pandora's daughter died as baby, or at least that's what she thought. But even if the kid ain't hers she won't put her in danger.'

'So, what's her plan?'

'Even if I did know, which I don't, I wouldn't tell you, Mr Blabbermouth,' she poked him in the chest accusingly. 'However, I did promise I would check Ciara is okay with my own two eyes, so you will be taking me to see her as thanks for keeping you safe tonight, Mr Wyatt.'

He scoffed, 'Keeping me safe?'

'I didn't see you getting a gun in there without me,' Pixie raised one brow.

'Okay, fine, I'm sure she'd be glad to see you anyway, she's still not talking to me,' he sighed.

'I don't blame her.'

Miles started up the car, pulling back onto the road. So, Pandora had knowingly played him. She knew he'd give her to Joey and she went along with it anyway, just to save Ciara. And he'd nearly screwed it up by mentioning Lila. But he was desperate, he needed to save Ciara and pleasing Joey was the only way. No matter the cost.

The relief when he'd seen Pandora alive was overwhelming, but he'd left her there in the devil's den. How long she'd stay alive was unsure. She seemed so calm and confident, almost content next to Joey. Was it all an act, or was there something else there that he didn't know?

Pandora's people were more than likely up to something, so the less he knew the better. He was done.

Pulling up at his house he went to open the car door, but Pixie was already up and out.

'We can drop the gentleman act now, Mr Wyatt,' she said, all the sweetness from the party truly gone.

She followed him into the house, as Jay came to the doorway to meet them.

'She hasn't spoken to me all night Boss,' Jay sighed, wishing they'd just sent Ciara away but she point-blank refused so keeping her close was the only option.

'CIARA!' Miles shouted, 'You've got a visitor.'

Silence.

'Which room is hers?' asked Pixie.

'Second on the right,' said Jay before Miles could answer.

Pixie glared at the pair as she passed them, storming up the stairs.

'Ciara, it's me Pixie,' she said knocking the door gently, 'Ciara, open up please.'

There was no reply. Pixie tried the handle, opening the door slowly.

'FUCK!' she shouted.

Miles and Jay raced up the stairs, meeting her in the doorway. As they glanced over her shoulder, they saw the open window.

Ciara was gone.

Thirty-Four

Safety off, Frankie stepped closer to the entrance. From the cameras, she couldn't tell who was banging on the entrance door to the club. If it was Joey's boys, that was never a welcome visit. As she got closer to the door the banging got louder.

'Frankie, are you there? Let me in. Please,' the voice pleaded.

Opening the door Frankie looked on in shock at the last person she thought she'd see darkening her door.

'Ciara, what are you doing here? You can't be here!'

'Please,' the tearful blonde begged, 'it's all my fault.'

Peeking her head out and looking around, she pulled the soaked skinny figure of Ciara inside.

'Ciara, if Miles finds you here, you'll bring a war to my door. I can't have that now; I've got too many people relying on me,' Frankie warned.

'But it's all my fault,' she sniffed.

Frankie begrudgingly guided her up to the office, taking her coat off her and grabbing her a towel as she tried to work out what to do with her.

'What the fuck!' Lila cursed as she walked in. 'She can't fucking be here!'

'I fucking know Lila, go check on the others, I'm dealing with it,' Frankie snapped.

Lila shook her head, muttering as she left.

Frankie sat down next to the sobbing Ciara.

'You can't stay here, Ciara, Miles will kill us. He only just got you back from Joey,' Frankie tried to explain.

'But it's all my fault,' she repeated again.

'What is?'

'Pandora.'

'Oh,' Frankie paused, realising. 'Ciara, that's not your fault. Pan knew exactly what she was doing sweetie.'

Ciara's face stopped leaking momentarily as her head shot up confused.

'Ciara, she gave herself up willingly to get you free. It was her idea.'

'But my brother...' Ciara stuttered.

'Did everything Pandora wanted him to, not that he quite knew that at the time,' chuckled Frankie, imagining the look on Miles's face when he realised he had been Pandora's pawn.

'But what do we do? We can't just leave her there,' Ciara begged. 'He's a fucking monster.'

Frankie smirked as the precious blonde cursed.

'We do nothing. You need to go home to your brother. We will deal with it.'

'No.'

'No?'

'I'm not going back until Pandora is safe and home,' Ciara stated with a clenched fist.

'And where are you going to stay?' Frankie laughed at the delusional princess.

'Here. I'm coming to work for you until Pandora returns,' Ciara replied.

Frankie almost choked but the look in Ciara's eyes told her she was deadly serious.

'Ciara, don't take this the wrong way but firstly, you've never had a job in your life, secondly, I'm not hiring and thirdly, your brother would never allow it.'

'Frankie...' Ciara paused with a sniff, 'firstly, you *are* giving me a job, secondly, I'm not leaving till Pandora is back safe and thirdly, I don't give a fuck what my brother thinks.'

Cursing twice in one night. The princess was growing a backbone. *What would Pandora do* thought Frankie. She knew exactly what she would have done. Pan would have given her a job and the opportunity to decide her own life.

The phone rang, pausing the conversation.

'Yes,' Frankie answered, 'I see...' She listened to the voice at the other end. 'She's here,' she said down the phone, 'yes I'm sure, she's sitting right in front of me.'

Ciara scowled as Frankie hung up.

'Was that my brother?'

'No, it was Pixie. But she and your brother are on the way over,' Frankie sighed. 'You wanna stay?' Ciara nodded brightly. 'Then you tell your brother to his face.'

Ciara's face dropped for a second, she gulped, 'Okay.'

'Okay?' Frankie asked.

'Yes, I'll tell him. Then you'll give me a job?'

'Deal.'

Frankie knew this would cause issues, but she also knew what Pandora would do in this situation. She just prayed Pandora was okay. Pixie had updated her on seeing Pandora, but nothing about the situation reassured her.

Fifteen minutes later, Lila reappeared with a sheepish-looking Pixie and a pissed-off Miles, before dipping back out of the office.

'Mr Wyatt, good to see you. Would you like a drink?' Frankie politely offered.

'No, I fucking don't. I want to know what the fuck you're doing with my sister,' he threatened, his hand closing in around Frankie's throat.

'I'm not doing anything with your sister,' Frankie smiled, 'unless you'd like me to. I didn't know you were into that kind of thing.'

Ciara blushed, shaking her head as Miles released his grip on Frankie's throat. Pixie watched on from the corner amused.

'Miles,' Ciara started, 'I came here.'

'But why?' He looked at his sister. 'You were safe at home.'

'But at what cost?' she demanded. 'You traded my life for another, my friend. You had no right!'

'You are my sister. I had every right!' he boomed, slamming his fist down onto the desk.

'No, you don't, you entitled jackass! You had no right!' Ciara screamed furiously.

'So, you're running away?' Miles said menacingly.

'I'm not running anywhere.'

'Kinda implied that when you snuck out of your bedroom window. I thought you'd been fucking kidnapped again!'

Ciara gulped, eyes down.

'I didn't mean to, I mean I didn't think,' she fought back the tears.

'That's it, you don't think. You forget who we are. You forget what we are. Come on, we are going home Ciara,' Miles beckoned.

'No.'

'What did you just say?'

'You heard me, brother,' Ciara replied calmly.

He stepped towards her, towering over her tiny frame.

'I will not be coming home until Pandora is free and safe.' It wasn't a threat, simply a statement.

'And where will you stay, my dear little sister?'

'Here.'

Miles's head snapped towards Frankie.

'And you're encouraging this?'

'Fuck am I, but I'm also not going to turn her away, it's not what Pan would want,' said Frankie simply.

'I could bring hell down on you,' he threatened.

'You could, but we wouldn't want Joey knowing how you double-crossed him at the docks now would we?' Frankie said sweetly.

It wasn't a card Frankie wanted to play but she needed to avoid war and bloodshed at the moment.

'Fine. But if so much as a hair on her head is hurt, I'm coming for you.'

He turned and stormed out followed by Pixie, who gave Ciara and Frankie a wink on the way out. Ciara's face lit up.

'Right,' said Frankie with a sigh, 'let's find you a job.'

Thirty-Five

'Dom, either say something or fuck off. I'm not in the mood,' Pandora growled as she stood looking out the bedroom window.

'Mia is asking for you.'

Pandora turned, following him down the corridor. It was 3 a.m. What was the child still doing awake?

Pandora wasn't allowed access to Mia without someone present, Dom had been put on supervision duty.

Pandora thought about Dom. He was loyal to Joey. Well, loyal was a strong word. Dom knew not to betray him but he also wasn't a complete jackass like most of Joey's men and had always done his best for Pan while not risking his neck. He wasn't stupid.

Opening the door, Dom nodded to Pan, letting her enter as he stayed outside with the nameless, voiceless guard. Most didn't talk to Pan unless necessary. Pandora encountered a visibly upset Mia. She couldn't call her daughter; she honestly didn't know if she was. That was a wound she wasn't prepared to open yet. But Mia was just a child and she would protect her as best she could, without getting too attached.

'You should be asleep,' she smiled, arms crossed.

'I can't sleep,' she sniffed, 'I heard screaming and I'm scared. Uncle Dom said it was a bad dream but it wasn't, I promise Mommy. Please don't let the monsters eat me!'

She raised an eyebrow to Dom whose blank face neither confirmed nor denied.

'Don't worry, I believe you,' Pandora reassured, tucking her back in with a soft kiss to the head. 'I'll go sort the monsters out, but you need sleep.'

'Yes Mommy,' Mia yawned, cuddling her bear.

Exiting the room, Pandora stormed off towards the basement, Dom hot on her heels.

'Pan! Not a good idea!'

'Do I look like I give a flying fuck?'

'He's busy Pan. You disturb him, you know what happens.'

'I know what used to happen. Past tense. What's he gonna do? Kill me?'

Dom grabbed her arm.

'Pan, I can't protect you this time,' he whispered.

Their eyes connected and she smiled softly. 'You don't have to Dom, I'm not that breakable little girl anymore. This bitch bites back now. Maybe it's time for me to rescue us both?'

She pulled her arm away, anger bubbling as she stormed into the room, the rotting stench attacking her nostrils.

'I'm busy,' Joey snapped. There was the monster she remembered.

Her heels scraped the concrete floor as she slowly trailed in.

'The child heard screaming.'

'So, what of it?' Joey replied, his back still to her.

'It scared her. She is a child.'

'She'll get over it.'

'Joey, she's your daughter...' Pandora knew she was poking the bear, looking for any hint of the lie being confirmed.

Joey stopped, rounding on her, giving her a full view of the guest. His face was unrecognisable from the shades of purples and reds that decorated it. The obvious aroma of piss radiated off him.

'Pandora,' Joey growled, 'I've been patient. I've been understanding.'

Pandora bit back a smirk.

'But you are starting to push your luck,' he grabbed her wrist tightly. 'You don't want to make me mad...'

'And you want me to be a good little girl, so no more dragging them through the house,' she smiled sweetly as if negotiating a lunch date.

He dropped her wrist. First point to Pandora.

She glanced again at the guest. His wheezing increasing, probably a collapsed lung. He tried to talk, to beg, but she knew he was already dead. He just hadn't stopped breathing yet.

'You trying to get intel?' she enquired.

'No, just reminding the world what happens when people fail me.'

The message was clear.

Pandora approached the poor fucker, his eyes so swollen she didn't think he could even see out of them. The guard next to him didn't meet her eyes, staring straight ahead.

She pulled his gun from his holster, taking off the safety and shooting the tortured man in the head. It was the smallest mercy she could afford.

Three guns snapped towards her.

Joey smirked.

'His breathing was annoying me,' she reasoned, handing the gun back to the guard who now glared at her.

Pandora stormed out of the basement before she gave in to the urge to put a bullet somewhere else.

This cage was growing tiresome.

Thirty-Six

'You're gonna wear a hole in the floor if you don't stop pacing Boss,' Jay joked.

'Fuck off Jay,' Miles snapped.

Miles didn't want Ciara with them. He didn't go to all that effort to rescue her for her to walk straight back into danger.

'She's a big girl, Boss,' Jay reasoned. 'You've kept her cooped up for too long. It's dangerous to shield someone like her for too long. She is vulnerable. Maybe being with them will give her some independence and teach her to look after herself.'

'She's my responsibility.'

'And you won't be around forever,' Jay threw back. 'What's she gonna do then? Look Boss,' he continued, 'I respect you and I'll follow you anywhere, but I'm also never going to lie to you. Ciara was bubble-wrapped and that was dangerous. I hate to admit it but she's probably in the best place at the minute.'

Miles didn't want to agree but he knew the smart-mouthed jackass was right.

'Where's Pixie?' Miles asked.

'Probably avoiding you,' Jay replied honestly.

Things had been awkward with Pixie but she never neglected her duties. She brought updates on Ciara to keep him appeased but avoided him wherever possible. He knew she must feel torn, working for the man who handed her friend over to a monster, but yet she stayed.

Miles's phone pinged.

'Fuck.'

'What's up, Boss?' Jay asked.

'Joey's having an auction and he's invited me.'

It wasn't an invite; it was a summons. Miles knew exactly what would be auctioned. His stomach turned. Drugs, weapons, violence... not a problem, he enjoyed those. But selling off young girls, that just didn't sit right with him. But if he didn't go, Joey could go after Ciara again.

'Go get Pixie,' Miles requested.

Moments later Jay returned with Pixie.

'You called for me, Mr Miles?' Her tone was still professional and courteous, and it irked him.

'Yes, we have another date to attend.'

'I'm sure I can get one of the girls to go with you...' she reasoned.

'No, unfortunately it needs to be you.' He paused. 'Joey is hosting an auction.'

Her face darkened and she nodded.

'I assume we are not there to shop?'

'Don't be stupid, I wouldn't be there at all if I didn't have too,' Miles sighed.

'Do you think Pan will be there?' Pixie asked.

'I have no idea,' he answered honestly.

'I hope not,' she muttered.

'Why?'

'Because I don't think she'd be able to stop herself from doing anything stupid.'

Miles hadn't thought about the loose cannon that was Pandora. How she was still alive was a mystery to him. He was sure Joey would have snapped her neck by now. What was he getting out of keeping her alive? So many unanswered questions; it made him uneasy.

He gave Pixie the details and she nodded, exiting the office to continue working. Miles ran his hands down his face.

God, he needed a drink.

Thirty-Seven

Pandora carefully twisted the curly red locks, finishing the second plait. Mia bounced off her lap grinning, spinning, her plaits swinging with her.

'Woah, slow down, you'll only make yourself dizzy,' Pandora chuckled.

'Looks like someone is enjoying motherhood.'

Pandora turned to see Joey leaning against the frame, his grin twisting her stomach. She ignored him, turning her attention back to Mia.

'Go with Uncle Dom, he'll sort you breakfast. He might even get you some of your favourite cereal!'

Mia nodded, racing out of the room to Dom who was stationed outside.

'I'm assuming you want something Joey,' she glared.

'From you?' he licked his lips slowly. 'Always, my firecracker. But this time I want you to come to me.'

'Not going to happen,' Pandora snapped, making a move to exit the room.

'Oh, but it will,' he said blocking the exit, pinning her against the door frame with one arm. 'You will come to me and you will make it convincing, and you know why.'

Mia

'But don't worry, we have all the time in the world this time Pan and you'll come around.'

He brushed his thumb over her bottom lip, his hand trailing softly down her arm. Taking her hand he lifted it to his lips placing a slow, lingering kiss to the back of her hand.

'But for now, I'm here to inform you that you are attending

an auction with me this afternoon and you will be on your best behaviour, so go get ready and look your best.'

He dropped her hand, releasing her as he walked away grinning. He was testing her. Waiting for her to step out of line. She couldn't stand by and watch as those poor girls were sold off like trash. She would gladly raise hell to stop that normally but she knew so much more was at stake this time.

She dragged herself off to where Dom and Mia were chuckling in the kitchen. She leant against the doorway watching as they sat, Mia eating her cereal and Dom nursing a piping hot coffee. His eyes glanced up, meeting hers.

'You knew about the auction?' It wasn't a question, more an accusation.

He nodded.

'A little heads-up maybe would have been appreciated,' she sighed.

'I didn't know he'd be taking you. You know he's banking on you doing something stupid so he can punish you,' Dom warned.

'Am I that predictable?' she smirked.

'Back then… yes. Now, not so much. He's trying to work out how far he can push you, how to break you.'

'Can't break something that's already broken,' Pandora reasoned. 'I suppose I better go get ready. You pair behave while I'm gone.'

'I always behave Mommy!' Mia gasped dramatically. 'It's Uncle Dom who's naughty,'

Shaking her head Pandora headed off to don her war makeup and prepare for the next round… After a scalding hot shower to remove Joey's touch.

***

After several slow hours, the dreaded knock came.

'Come in,' Pandora responded, slipping into her silver heels.

'He's waiting,' Dom informed her.

'Of course he is.'

Dom escorted her down to the car, opening the door for her to enter. It was the first time she had left the house since her arrival. She forced herself not to try and bolt.

As she sat down, the door shut, leaving her next to the monster.

'I don't need to remind you,' Joey purred, placing a grip on her thigh, 'best behaviour tonight my dear. Do you understand?'

She didn't respond, refusing to meet his gaze as she looked out the window. He squeezed harder.

'I said do you understand?' he growled.

'Yes. I heard you the first time, Joey,' she seethed, tempted to try and remove his iron grip.

'Good girl,' he smiled, sending a queasy shudder through her body. If any other male had said that it might have almost been sexy, but from him it was more like a threat. There was only one response her body had ever given Joey and that was disgust.

Joey's eyes didn't leave her, scanning up and down her body, his grip loosened, his fingers now circling her knee.

'You may not know it now my dear Pan,' his eyes darkened with a hunger she recognised, 'but soon enough, you'll be begging for my touch. I bet you're wet right now just thinking about all the things I'll do to you as you scream my name.'

Joey was delusional and as compliant as she was trying to be, her tongue was off its leash.

'Joey,' Pandora paused, grinning, 'you make me about as dry as the fucking Sahara Desert, you can check if you want,' she offered, 'but the only time your name will roll off my lips in pleasure is as I gut you and bathe in your blood because let's be honest, that's the only way you're going to make me wet.'

Her head smashed into the car door as his hand connected to her face. Her grin widened as she wiped the blood from the corner of her lip.

'There we go,' she chuckled. 'Now *there's* the Joey I remember.'

'Don't push me, Pandora!' Joey warned. 'Look what you made me do! You just can't help yourself. Well don't worry, we'll discuss this later.'

Pandora knew there was very little to discuss and punishment would be coming. As the car pulled up to the abandoned factory, she straightened her dress before stepping out, proudly wearing the red mark across her face. A sign of how Joey treats his toys, the sting a welcome reminder of everything she was working for.

Joey gently placed an arm around her waist leading her into the building.

Thirty-Eight

'No hero stunts,' Miles warned.

'Do I look like an idiot?' Pixie snapped back.

'We are here to turn up, show our faces then leave as soon as we can, understand?'

'Yes, Boss! I will watch all the poor women sold off like trash like a good girl and smile with the sleazy fucks.'

'Pixie...' he grumbled.

'I know! Can we just get this over with?'

As they exited the car, Miles saw the instant shift in Pixie's body language and face. The serious pissed off look had vanished, replaced by the meek, giggly hostess. They entered the old factory, greeted by Joey's men who led them to the auction area.

He could see Pixie glancing around doe-eyed, he knew it was a ruse to scope out the place. He couldn't afford for her to do anything stupid though or they'd both be dead.

Along the left wall were ten figures. Ten haunted sets of eyes. Ten girls to be auctioned. Men were inspecting them, touching them, devouring them with their eyes. Most seemed to be over eighteen, thankfully, but one was definitely much younger; blonde hair, she reminded him of a younger Ciara. He shook himself, tearing his gaze away.

'See anything you like Miles?' Joey chuckled as he approached with Pandora on his arm.

'You know this isn't my cup of tea, Mr Siegel,' he replied honestly.

Both Pixie and Miles noticed the reddening of Pandora's cheek and the small cut on her lip as she smirked at both of them. Obviously, obedience wasn't something that came naturally to Pandora.

'I'm always telling him he should broaden his horizons, Mr Siegel,' Pixie piped in, her eyes trailing over the girls with a glint.

'See Miles, you should listen to your gorgeous companion here. She sees the bigger picture,' Joey taunted, leading Pandora off.

Before Miles could say a word, Pixie was trailing up and down the line of girls with a hungry look in her eyes, stroking their faces, circling each one like she was ready to devour them. Miles's stomach clenched uneasily as he watched her effortlessly assume the character she had chosen for the day.

As the auction started, Pandora had to push back the constant flow of bile as she watched helplessly as each girl was paraded up front to be sold. Some were silent, resolved to their fates, some crying and pleading, others shaking uncontrollably in the less than warm attire they were clothed in.

But what Pandora did do was memorize the faces of each fucker that bought a girl. Storing it away for a later date.

The last girl was brought up to auction. They'd saved the best till last. The youngest.

The bidding shot up quickly, as did the panic in the girl's eyes. Pandora twitched, looking at escape routes and possible ideas. None would end in anything but death.

'£100,000!' came an excited squeak.

Pandora and Miles both snapped their heads towards Pixie who was grinning like a Cheshire cat as she placed her first bid, double what had come before for the other girls.

The room was in shocked silence, and the hammer fell. Pixie bounced in her seat, as the tears rolled down the poor girl's face.

'I thought we weren't shopping,' Miles casually dropped.

'Oh you know me Boss, when I see something I like, I just have to have it.' She smirked. He wasn't buying it.

'I assume you have £100,000 to pay for it?' He raised an eyebrow.

'No, but you're going to buy her for me for being such a good girl,' she purred suggestively, loud enough so the old fat fuck next to them needed to readjust his sitting position.

Miles sighed. 'Suppose I'll pay so you can collect your new toy.'

He offered her a hand to help her up from her seat. The pair sauntered over to the payment and collection point, where Pandora and Joey were waiting.

'I must say Miles, your young lady friend here is quite impressive,' he applauded, 'If you ever want to let her go, I'd be happy to find her a place here with me.'

Pixie blushed. 'You're too kind Mr Siegel, but Mr Wyatt here keeps me plenty busy.' She wiggled her eyebrows.

Pandora's face was stone and she refused to speak. Joey ignored her as he continued.

'Well, I hope you enjoy your purchase. We'll be down to the club soon to see how she's settling in.'

'Oh, she's not for the club,' Pixie interrupted, licking her lips, 'she's for me.'

Joey loosened his collar, parting his lips as he kept his gaze on Pixie, the dark hooded look deepening as he realised her implication.

'Well in that case then, enjoy,' he replied with a smile, leading Pandora away.

They approached the small blonde, tears freely flowing down her face as her body tremored and her eyes refused to look anywhere but the floor. Miles settled the bill, while Pixie took off her coat and placed it round her. The guard next to her raised an eyebrow. Pixie squared up to him.

'Well, she's no use to me if she catches a chill and dies is she you idiot?'

He backed down, eyes following as he muttered an apology.

'Mr Wyatt,' she said lazily, 'can you carry the shopping? We haven't got all day.'

Miles, getting the hint, scooped the girl up, coat still wrapped round her as they exited towards the car. As Jay stepped out to open the doors, Miles locked eyes with him sending a clear warning not to say a thing. Pixie almost skipped to the car.

'Look, Jay, we went shopping… do you like?' she asked lightly.

'Yeah… good choice,' Jay replied.

Placing the girl in the back with Pixie, Miles hopped in the front with Jay, who pulled out of the drive looking clueless.

The girl sat, coat draped over her as Pixie leaned over her to pull her belt on. She flinched. Pixie didn't say a word.

They weren't in the clear yet.

Thirty-Nine

Fists clenched, Pandora bit the inside of her cheek until the coppery taste of blood filled her mouth. Using the pain, she distracted herself from the hand stroking her thigh and the face staring at her that she dreamt of smashing to pieces as the car drove them away from the auction.

'Did you enjoy your little outing my dear?' Joey chuckled.

Pandora held her silence.

'I asked you a question.'

'Joey, you aren't going to like a word that comes out of my mouth so best I keep it shut.' She wasn't stupid, but she wasn't a scared little girl anymore. She wasn't going to lose herself, not this time.

'I'm sure there's other ways I can put that mouth to good use,' he whispered in her ear as he nibbled her lobe, adjusting his trousers with his free hand.

'Not unless you want surgery afterwards,' Pandora warned.

'I'm getting a little tired of this hard-to-get act Pan.'

'That would imply it's an act.'

'I'm sure we can come up with some way to motivate you…' his tone warned.

She knew there was only so long his patience would last. He wanted her to come to him willingly, the ultimate sign of defeat. But if he couldn't get that he'd coerce her to get what he wanted. She knew she couldn't refuse but she knew it would break her to do it.

Once back at the house Joey took his leave to attend to business in the basement. Pandora followed the sounds of giggles to find Dom and Mia baking cookies.

'I'm not sure if there is more dough on the tray or on you pair,' Pandora giggled.

They stopped, looking up, caught red handed. Dom's eyes met Pandora's and he frowned.

'I take it you pushed,' he said approaching her to inspect her face.

'Looks worse than it is,' she shrugged.

'I told you not to push him,' he sighed.

'You know me, just can't help myself.'

'You are going to get yourself killed Pan,' he warned.

'I need you to do something for me Dom,' she whispered, as Mia played around with the cookie cutters, creating shapes.

'You know I can't get you out of here,'

'I know. I need you to promise me that if anything happens, you'll protect her. If you can get her out, there's somewhere I need you to take her.'

Pandora took her finger, writing carefully in the flour dust on the counter.

'Memorise this Dom,' her hand lingered for a few moments before wiping all the evidence.

'I can't promise anything,' he answered honestly.

'I know.'

But she knew he'd try. He always did.

'Right little one,' Pandora said, 'we need to get you cleaned up. Uncle Dom will clean up this mess as he helped make it!'

Mia stuck her tongue out at Dom who returned the gesture as Pan scooped up the mucky child, covering them both in flour and dough.

After Mia had been cleaned up and tucked in for the night, Pandora headed back to the room. Joey was waiting.

'Did you enjoy your afternoon with your daughter?' he teased.

'You still haven't proved to me that she's mine,' Pandora challenged.

'She's yours. You know that.'

Pandora still wasn't convinced but it changed nothing; the child was innocent. As she changed into her nightclothes in the bathroom the feeling of dread grew. Joey had been laying hints all day.

As she exited the ensuite, he stood in the doorway. His hand softly trailed from her arm to round her back pulling her in closer, their bodies now touching as she could feel the strain from his trousers threatening to break free. A traitorous tear escaped as she cursed herself. She was still weak; she was still broken and this time she didn't think she could piece herself back together.

'Hush my little firecracker, I can make this as pleasurable or painful as you want. The choice is yours,' he whispered as he softly kissed her collar, his hands now circling her lower back.

The tears trickled, as Joey wiped them from her cheek.

'No need for tears, not yet at least,' he teased.

It was taking every ounce of self-restraint she had not to try and kill him there and then. He guided her towards the bed, lying her down gently. She clenched her eyes and her thighs shut, her body tensing as he straddled, raising her hands, pinning them above her head. Pandora felt his heavy breath, towering over her face.

'Eyes open, Pandora.'

It wasn't a request.

She opened them, faced with his dark eyes. Memories came flooding back – his touch, his kiss, the things he had done to her and made her do. She refused to shed another tear.

She stared at him blankly, relaxing her body. She would not give him a reaction; she would not give him the pleasure of knowing the fear he placed in her soul and the nightmares he had haunted for years.

Brushing his nose along her neck, he teased his tongue along her earlobe. Pulling back, he devoured her with his eyes, ready to attack her lips.

Lowering himself, grinning, he descended on her lips as she fought not to close her eyes again.

As his lips touched hers, he jerked upwards.

Shots rang out.

'What the fuck!' Joey shouted racing out of the room, snatching his gun from the bedside table.

Forty

Pandora jumped to her feet; barefoot she ran. 'DOM!!!' she screamed.

Moments later she ran into Dom in the corridor, both heading for the same direction.

Mia's room.

'Gun, now!' Pandora demanded as shots flew. Whoever this was they didn't care about collateral.

Joey had lots of enemies but she'd never known any of them to attack his home. How the fuck had they got in? This might have been an inside job but she didn't have time to play detective.

Dom handed her his spare and they swept down the corridor in unison.

'Since when did you become so comfortable with a gun?' he asked over his shoulder as they approached the corridor next to Mia's.

'I told you, I'm not the girl you knew before Dom.'

'I'm seeing that,' he grinned as his eyes swept up and down her in her nightclothes, still barefoot. She rolled her eyes, before her mouth dropped. One shot.

A body dropped behind Dom.

'You wanna focus?' she snapped.

'Yes, Boss,' he saluted.

The shouts and shots continued. Two figures came running round the corner. Three shots popped. Two bodies dropped.

'FUCK!'

'You okay Pan?' Dom turned to see the flood of blood.

'I'm fine, just got my arm. Let's go!' she hissed, clutching her left upper arm with her right hand as the blood trickled through.

They got to Mia's door; Dom cracked it open peaking inside. It looked empty. Pandora's heart plummeted. They'd got her!

Dom, ignoring Pandora's panic, knelt down at the wall beside Mia's bed, knocking on it. The wall cracked open, revealing a small head of red poking out.

'Uncle Dom, did I win?' Mia grinned.

Pandora, whose heart was still trying to brutally escape her chest, looked confused.

'Mia is super good at our favourite game, aren't you Mia?' Dom said slowly as Mia grinned nodding. 'If Mia ever hears the loud bangs it means the game has started and she has to hide until I come find her, and she won!'

'Mommy, are you okay?' Mia said sadly, as she saw Pandora's bloody arm.

'Yes sweetie I just fell over playing a game with Uncle Dom, I'm fine,' Pandora reassured her, starting to feel dizzy from the waves of pain attacking her.

Turning her attention to Dom she knew what she had to do.

'Dom…'

'I see that look, Pan, you want to do something stupid. Don't you dare.'

'Remember, Dom.'

***

Joey was pissed. Who the fuck was stupid enough to come into his house and try to kill him? He spat on the body twitching below him, stamping on the unrecognisable face; rage had taken over.

As his breathing calmed, he scoped the house. Four of his men dead, three injured. No sight of Dom or Pandora.

He knew exactly where Pandora would be.

'Lex! Come with me. Kane find me someone alive, I want fucking answers! Everyone else get this place cleaned up!'

Joey approached Mia's room with Lex, both guns at the ready. Silence was unnerving, he was waiting for one of the leftovers to jump out. They passed two bodies in the hall, lifeless and bloody. Joey reached the handle and turned.

Blood pooled on the unicorn rug of Mia's room. Joey located the source of the blood.

Pandora.

Lifeless.

Approaching her slowly, he looked for signs of a trap. Lex knelt down feeling her neck.

'She's alive, Boss. But she's lost a fuck ton of blood.'

Pandora was shot, Mia was gone and Dom was missing too. Joey wanted answers and he wanted them yesterday.

***

Pain shot through her arm, her shoulder feeling like it had been wrenched from the socket. The room came into focus. She was back in bed. The bed where he had almost…

As she tried to move, the pain immobilised her. Glancing down from her position, her clothes had been changed and her arm bandaged. Pandora recalled the events. The invasion, the shoot-out, Mia and Dom, darkness.

The door opened and in walked a dark and dangerous monster. A pissed off Joey.

'Mia…' Pandora croaked, 'Is she okay?'

'What do you remember?' he asked sitting on the edge of the bed next to her, bringing a glass of water to her lips. A few drops escaped her chin and Joey wiped them off gently.

'Shots,' she replied. 'I went to find Mia. I think I was shot. I remember getting to her room, but she wasn't there. Joey, tell me, is she okay?'

'Did you see Dom?'

'No. Joey tell me. Is she okay?' Pandora begged.

'She's missing.'

'What do you mean she's missing?' Panic rose in her chest.

'Exactly what I said Pan, she's missing,' his voice betrayed no hint of emotion.

'You said nobody knew about her, you said she was a secret Joey. Why would they take her?' Pandora cried.

'Nobody knew about her, I made sure of it but if they came across her, they've probably taken her thinking she is important,' he shrugged.

'She is fucking important, Joey, she's your daughter,' Pandora screamed trying to lift herself up, launching herself at him.

'We made one, we can always make another. I'm more concerned they've taken Dom. He knows too much that could cost me money,' he mused, pushing her back down.

'You fucking cunt! That is our child, your child. She is not expendable!'

'Everyone is expendable my dear. Even you if needs must,' he stated, standing to leave the room. 'Get some rest, Firecracker, I'm not done with you yet,' he smirked as the door closed.

Pandora lay still, recalling the events over and over until sleep took hold and she welcomed the escape from the throbbing pain in her heart and her shoulder.

Forty-One

As they pulled up at Limbo, Pixie looked at the girl sat next to her. She hadn't spoken a word. Pixie hadn't either. This had to be done right.

'You sure about this, Pixie?' Miles asked warily.

'Well I'm not taking her to yours. Joey thinks I'm keeping her to myself, so this is the best option.'

The girl, who looked like she was completely zoned out didn't react to their conversation. Jay went to get out of the car.

'Jay, stay. I'll handle it,' Pixie demanded.

'I quite like it when you get bossy,' he grinned.

Pixie rolled her eyes, getting out of the car and opening the door on the opposite side. She gently undid the seat belt, softly taking the girl's hands and guiding her out with the coat still draped around her. The fear in the girl's eyes was like a sucker punch to Pixie but she'd had no choice. Hopefully, she hadn't caused any further trauma.

Miles got out of the car, followed by Jay.

'Don't worry, I'm only coming to see Ciara,' Miles said defensively.

Pixie nodded, leading the girl to the entrance. She didn't try to fight or resist. The poor child was broken, but hopefully repairable.

Frankie greeted them at the door with a groan.

'Do I even want to know?' said Frankie hand to head.

'Pixie went shopping,' joked Jay.

Pixie turned with a swing, her fist connecting with his jaw.

'Shut the fuck up, you insensitive twat!' she snapped.

'Sorry,' he muttered rubbing his face. Miles glared at him as they followed Frankie in.

'I'm just here to check in with Ciara,' Miles said to Frankie.

'CIARA!' Frankie hollered, 'Your bro is here.'

Ciara poked her head out from behind the bar and he noticed her hair up in a messy bun. She was wearing a crop top, baggy jeans and trainers.

'Who are you and what have you done with my sister?' he said scratching his head. She certainly didn't look like the pampered princess he'd left here. She playfully punched him in the arm.

'Right, I'll leave you lot to it,' interrupted Pixie. 'Frankie, shall we?'

Frankie nodded. 'LILA,' she hollered once more, 'OFFICE, NOW!'

'No need to scream, I'm not deaf!' groaned Lila from the DJ booth where she'd pulled her headphones off. The three led the young girl up to the office. She followed obediently, still silent. Pixie led her to the sofa and sat her down.

'So...' Frankie began.

'There was an auction...' Pixie started, 'and I couldn't leave her there, she was the youngest by far. I couldn't get them all out, but I couldn't leave her.'

'So you kidnapped her?' Lila asked.

'No, I bought her,' Pixie said meekly, a small flash of fear spread across the girl's face.

'How did you afford to do that?' Frankie gasped.

'I made Mr Wyatt pay...'

'And he agreed?' Lila's shocked tone interrupted again.

'Didn't really give him a choice,' Pixie smiled. It was a small form of revenge for his betrayal, but it made her smile that she'd made his pockets hurt at least.

Lila sat on the sofa keeping her distance, speaking as softly as she could. 'Do you have a name, my lovely?'

The girl looked at Lila, the first eye contact she'd made.

'Florence,' she stammered, 'but people used to call me Flo.'

The tears started to flow as she spoke.

'It's okay Flo, we're not going to hurt you,' Lila reassured her, edging a fraction closer.

'But the lady,' she glanced at Pixie. 'They said I belonged to whoever bought me.'

'You belong to nobody,' Pixie snapped. 'Not me, not them, nobody.'

'But you paid £100,000 for me,' Flo sniffed uneasily.

'It was the only way to get you out of there safely,' Pixie explained.

'I can't pay you back though,' the panic was clear in her face.

'You don't have to. Do you have any family Flo?'

She shook her head silently.

'Well you do now,' Frankie piped in.

'Lila, can you take Flo here to get checked over by Felix and then we can work out a plan of action?' Pixie asked.

Lila nodded, coaxing the girl out of the office, keeping Pixie's warm coat wrapped round her.

'There's some spare clothes downstairs as well Lila,' Frankie called. 'Get her in something more... appropriate and warm.' Lila nodded over her shoulder.

'You love bringing me complications, Pixie,' Frankie sighed, grabbing two glasses.

'What was I supposed to do? Pandora was there too. I could see she was about to do something, I had to,' Pixie reasoned.

'How did she look? Did she say anything?'

Pixie shook her head. 'Nope, but she was sporting a nice mark across her face and a split lip.'

'For fuck's sake. This is killing me leaving her there, Pixie,' Frankie shook her head, downing her drink in one go, followed by Pixie.

'What's that Frankie?' Pixie said pointing to the cameras behind Frankie's head.

Frankie's head spun round, bringing up the camera in question. There at the secure entrance was a hooded figure, holding something in their arms.

'Nobody knows about that entrance, Frankie.'

'Tell me something I don't know.' Frankie snapped. 'Let's go. Grab the boys, I smell trouble.'

Forty-Two

Frankie opened the door outwards as the lads positioned themselves approaching from outside. They caged in the visitor; guns all trained on him. He still held onto whatever was in his arms.

'Shush,' he whispered, unfazed by the guns. 'You'll wake her.'

Pixie pushed past Frankie to get a better look.

'Dom?' she said quietly, recognising him from the party.

'Hey Pixie, any chance we can get her inside, out the cold?' Dom asked softly with a smile.

'Who?' Frankie asked confused.

'Mia,' Dom replied, lifting the blanket in his arms slightly to reveal a head of red hair.

Ignoring everyone, Pixie ushered them inside, much to Frankie's dismay.

'Take him straight downstairs,' Frankie ordered.

'I go where she goes,' Dom said flatly.

Frankie paused inside the door, not wanting him in any further but not wanting the sleeping child out in the cold.

'How the fuck did you find this entrance?' Frankie demanded, resisting the urge to point a gun at him with the child in his arms.

'Pandora,' he explained. 'I promised her I would protect Mia and she gave me these co-ordinates. I couldn't get her out this time but I could at least get Mia out.'

'This time?' Frankie quizzed.

'Yes, I helped Pandora escape the first time. This time I've signed my own death warrant.'

'Shall we take this to somewhere more comfortable and child friendly?' Pixie suggested as the child began to stir in his arms.

Heading down into the club, to the VIP booths, Miles spied the group and his eyes lit with fire as he saw Dom. He launched towards him.

'What the fuck is he doing here? He's Joey's mutt!' Miles snapped, still barging towards him when a sound stopped him in his tracks.

A shrill scream left the bundle in Dom's arms as she woke to the near stampede of Miles.

'Can we tone down the testosterone and not upset the child?' Pixie snarled.

'He can't be here!' Miles demanded.

'Well he is, so get over it!' Pixie snapped, squaring up to Miles.

'He's going to tell Joey everything and get us all fucking killed slowly!' Miles growled, as Jay eyed Dom warily.

Dom, who was cuddling the now fully awake child sat down, still holding her.

'First, can we stop swearing please?' he asked politely. 'Secondly, I don't belong to Joey, never have done. I was trapped just as much as anyone. Pandora gave me an out with Mia and I took it as promised. The only thing keeping Pandora there and compliant was Mia. When the house was attacked last night, we used the chaos for me and Mia to slip out so they would think whoever attacked took us. I have no idea who was stupid enough to hit Joey's but it caused mayhem'

'You left Pandora there!' Pixie shrieked.

'I made a promise,' he replied. 'If she came too then Joey would smell a rat, plus she was shot so she wouldn't have gotten far. It took me hours to walk here carrying Mia.'

'SHOT?' Pixie snapped. 'You could have started with that!'

'She'll be fine, it was in the arm and it will make things look more convincing to Joey,' he reassured her.

'I'm gonna ask what we all wanna know,' Frankie muscled in. 'Is she Pandora's?'

'We don't know,' replied Dom, 'but Pandora felt it didn't matter and I agree.'

Miles's phone rang.

'Everyone shut up! Keep the kid silent too,' he glared at Dom who smiled at Mia putting a finger to his lips as she nodded.

Miles answered, 'Yes Mr Siegel,' the room collectively held a breath. 'When?' He waited for the reply, 'Yes, I understand.'

The phone clicked off.

'And…' Pixie asked, hand on hip.

'He was attacked, doesn't know who yet. Wants to borrow some of my men for extra security as he lost a few… and he wants me to find who took Dom and get him back.'

Dom shifted uneasily.

'No mention of Mia?' he asked.

'No,' Miles replied. 'Jay, you know who to grab, go play house with Joey. Get a discreet update on Pandora if you can but don't do anything risky.'

'Of course, Mr Wyatt won't risk anything for anyone other than himself,' Pixie spat.

'I won't risk a war we can't win Pixie, stop being emotional,' Miles tried to reason.

'Emotional? Says a man! The species who think with their crotch not their brain,' she scoffed.

Jay shook his head at the pair, 'I'm just going to back away and go leave you two to it…'

'Uncle Dom,' Mia said sweetly, 'when is Mommy coming?'

The room all looked at the small child, whose red locks and small face reminded them so much of her.

'Soon sweetie, I promise, soon,' Dom replied.

Forty-Three

Voices filled the corridor. New voices.

Pandora strained to hear; she didn't want to move too much in case Joey realised she was healing faster than he thought. She knew what was coming as soon as she was healed.

A soft knock came on the door.

'Come in,' she called.

A familiar cheeky smile appeared around the door.

'Jay?' she whispered. 'What are you doing here?'

'Joey demanded Miles send extra men to cover for the dead ones he lost. Don't worry, Joey is out on business and my boys are on your door. We can talk.'

Pandora eyed him warily. Talk. Sounded like a trap.

'What would you like to talk about Jay?' she smiled sweetly.

'Well, we could talk about the weather,' he teased, 'or about how sexy I am. But I thought you'd prefer to talk about the package that turned up at Limbo.'

The breath she was holding escaped. Thank fuck they made it.

'I'm not sure what you mean.'

He nodded, realising she was wary.

'It's okay Pandora, I understand. I'm not sure how long we are here covering for. I'm under orders not to intervene or do anything stupid but I'm sure sending a message back would be alright.'

'I've got nobody to send a message to,' Pandora replied. The risk was too great. Miles had only betrayed her for Ciara, but what was to say Joey didn't have Ciara again?

Jay nodded. 'Just to let you know Pixie is getting antsy, I wouldn't be surprised if she stormed the place single handed to come get you soon,' he smiled, 'she's definitely a one of a kind.'

Pandora smiled too. She didn't want anyone getting hurt for her. But now Mia was gone, the carrot was too. Joey thought he had her trapped but the cage was an illusion. Pandora just needed the right opportunity now.

Jay left her with her thoughts and picked up his phone. Pandora listened from the door.

'Hey Pixie, just to let you know that package you wanted me to check on, yeah that one. It's okay, just a bit ruffled, but okay,' he paused, listening. 'No it's not ready for collection yet, you know what Mr Wyatt said. I'll let you know if anything changes.'

The conversation ended.

She couldn't risk trusting Jay, but he already seemed to know everything. Pandora was torn. Jay wasn't one of hers. She needed time to think.

When Joey came in to check on her later, she made sure she was the fragile injured little Pan. He groaned, moaning about how long it was taking for her to heal. She knew his patience would eventually run out, but she needed to drag this out as long as she could.

From the conversations she'd heard, Joey had no leads on who had ordered the hit. The guests in the basement were tight-lipped, which was impressive considering what Joey's boys were probably putting them through. The longer it took him to find who did it, the better protected Dom and Mia would be. Frankie would make sure they were safe.

***

Over the coming days, more of Miles's men were stationed at the house. Jay kept popping in when Joey was out to try and convince Pandora of his intentions, but Pandora was still tight lipped.

He decided to change tactic. Walking into her room, he handed her a phone. Taking it warily like it was about to explode, she listened to the voices at the other end.

'Boss, can you hear me?' Frankie's voice came through clear across the line.

'Frankie...' Pandora's voice cracked.

'Miles doesn't know Jay's rung, he's not wanting to risk Joey's wrath, so we don't have long.'

Pandora's eyed flickered to the cheeky *I told you so* wink from Jay.

'Is Mia okay?' Pandora asked warily.

Dom's voice echoed down the phone, 'She's fine Pan. We both are.'

The tears streamed freely now.

There was a knock at the door. 'Jay, he's on his way back,' the voice came.

Jay hung up the phone, leaving the room without a word. Wiping the tears, she fought to pull herself together.

Ten minutes later a car tore across the gravel drive, and doors began slamming. Smashing and crashing bounced over the house as Joey cursed and shouted, obviously still no closer to finding out who attacked him. He stormed into the bedroom, his eyes locked onto Pandora, fire and fury burning through him.

Without a word he grabbed her by her shirt, pulling her out of the bed. He twisted her around, bending her over forcefully. She held onto her injured arm which burnt, her arms crushed underneath her.

Panic shot through her as she felt him push up against her, a sob catching in her throat as she heard the zip lowering.

There were no words, he didn't tell her to shush, no offers of pain or pleasure. She had run out of time. There was only one option. She tried to lift up only be forced back down. Again, she tried, her fingers now digging into the stitches on her arm as she tried to resist. The more she resisted the more he hardened against her, chuckling at her despair and panic. She could feel his arousal growing as her fear and pain increased.

Tearing her fingers into her stitches she felt the warm pool of blood leaking out onto the satin sheets. Pain flooded through her, but it was pain of her choosing. She still had some control as she slipped into unaware blissful darkness.

***

As she woke, Jay towered over her grinning.

'Well, that was one way...' he chuckled

'Did he...' she whispered, not trusting herself to finish the sentence.

'Nope, but you pissed him off, apparently he wants you awake for that,' he laughed. 'He stormed out demanding someone come stitch you back up.'

'But who?' She looked down at her fresh clothes.

'I did. I thought you'd prefer to wake up in something fresh and comfortable. I promise I didn't peek much,' he teased.

'Fuck you, Jay.'

'Maybe later. You need to rest for now. Take these,' he said handing her the painkillers and water, 'I'll bring you some food later.'

'Thank you,' she muttered, slipping back into sleep.

Forty-Four

Joey didn't visit again and Pandora was grateful for the reprieve, no matter how painful it had been to get. But his lack of presence meant he was out looking for Dom, which also left Mia in danger.

Jay hadn't rung anyone again for her and she hadn't asked. It wasn't worth the risk. But she longed to hear their voices and know that they were okay.

There had still been no leads; someone knew something, but nobody was opening up to Joey no matter how much blood he'd shed and the bodies were mounting up. If Joey had been dangerous before, he'd hit a whole new level and nobody was safe, including his own men.

Joey had called a meeting of all his men and Miles had been summoned with his men too. The unease in the air was stifling and everyone was waiting for the explosion. Joey was a ticking time bomb. Even his closest men were on edge. Him shooting one in the head for questioning him didn't help.

Pandora could hear the cars pulling up and the hum of conversation. Too many of them in one place. Joey was planning something and it wasn't good. She was scratching round the edges of her uneven, itchy stitches when Jay popped his head in.

'You okay?' he asked.

'Yeah, just dandy,' she drawled, 'any idea what's going on?'

'They don't tell me anything. I just know that yesterday Joey sent out a summons for everyone. I think he's about to go to war.'

'With who?' Pandora asked.

'Everyone. He's paranoid and convinced everyone is plotting against him. They probably are to be fair. He's cracking and it's not like he was the most stable in the first place,' Jay reasoned. 'I'll be outside the door if you need anything.' He closed the door softly leaving Pandora with her thoughts.

It felt like she'd been trapped at Joey's for a lifetime. Her biggest fear in life was being locked in a cage and she knew that she wouldn't survive it much longer, it was by sheer luck she had managed to dodge him so far. But her luck would run out and the darkness would consume her once more.

The noise of cars arriving stopped and the mass of footsteps slowed. The meeting had started. Pandora couldn't hear Joey's voice from the bedroom, but Jay had one of Miles's boys close enough to listen in and report back later.

The clock slowed, time torturously dragging, tick by tick by tick. Pandora stretched, confident that Joey would be occupied for a while. Pacing the room, she grabbed fresh night clothes and, slipping her feet into her slippers, headed to the bathroom to brush her teeth. Looking in the mirror she didn't recognise the figure looking back. Her treasured silky locks were fuzzy and wild. Her skin pale and her eyes darkened by the circles that decorated them. As she stared, a figure appeared in the mirror behind her. Jay's face told her something had happened.

'Pan, we have a situation.'

Spinning round, she recognised the familiar noise of gunfire. But who and what was still unclear. Was Joey cleaning house, or was this another attack?

Pulling a gun out, Jay approached her, reaching his hand out to pass her the weapon.

'No time to change,' he said, glancing up and down at her nightclothes, silk shorts and a button up silk shirt with soft slippers.

'Seems I'm making a habit of shoot outs in my PJs,' she half laughed. 'Maybe this time I can avoid getting shot. I think I'm running out of lives.'

Lenny and Sparky were positioned outside the door. Both nodded to Pandora as she exited the room with Jay. None of them explained what was going on, but the sounds of bullets were coming from every direction.

Jay led the way as they cleared the corridors one by one. They turned the corner to be faced with a masked intruder. Lenny took aim but Pandora shoved him, sending his bullet into a nearby wall.

'What the fuck Pan?' shouted Jay.

'Look you idiot,' snapped Pan. 'She ain't even aiming at you!'

'She?' Jay's confused face scrunched up as he looked again. Lenny and Sparky still had their guns aimed.

The mask lifted. 'You wouldn't shoot lil' old me would you Jay?' She winked.

'Pixie, for fucks sake, we could have shot you!' Jay groaned.

'That would require you to be able to hit a target first,' she teased blowing a kiss at Lenny who blushed.

'Right, come on we've got work to do,' she said grabbing four masks and a set of overalls out of her holdall and throwing them at Jay.

Pandora's face lit up with a grin and she grabbed one of the masks and the overalls off Jay.

'Don't suppose you've got some trainers in that bag Pixie?' Pandora asked, but Pixie shook her head.

'I can't think of everything, Boss. I wasn't betting on you being ready for a nap!' Pixie rolled her eyes.

'Fuck it, I'll make do,' Pandora replied.

It was time to play.

Forty-Five

Miles couldn't tell who was shooting who anymore as he ducked for cover. Joey had summoned all his men here, plus all of Miles's men too. Most of Miles's men had been dotted about on security detail, while Joey addressed his own.

He'd demanded answers, he'd demanded results. What he hadn't demanded was a full-on invasion.

'What the fuck Miles!' Joey shouted across the room. 'Where are your fucking men?'

'All fucking dead by the sounds of it, thanks to you dragging me into your little crusade Joey!' Miles shouted back above the gunfire.

'When we get out of here, I'm going to fucking rip that fucking tongue out of your head Miles!' Joey threatened.

'Maybe focus on staying alive first,' Miles smirked before making a dash for better cover.

'Miles! Get the fuck back here!' Joey screamed.

Miles didn't look back. Diving for the doorway, he narrowly escaped a bullet as he took a breath and pushed himself up against a wall. Turning to move, he felt it before he saw it. The hard rim of the gun now pushed against his head.

He wouldn't grovel.

'Any last words Mr Wyatt?' the familiar voice purred.

'Pandora?' He spun round; the gun now squarely planted on his forehead. As he glanced down, he smirked at the fluffy footwear his captor was modelling.

'Don't say a word,' she threatened.

'It's hard to feel scared with such offensive footwear presented to me,' he said, glancing at the masked figures surrounding her.

A knee connected to his crotch with force.

'Okay,' he groaned painfully, 'I deserved that.'

'Where is he?' she asked.

'Dining room, far side,' Miles replied, rubbing his bruised manhood.

'You coming?' she asked.

'Wouldn't miss it,' he answered, taking a mask from Pixie with a grin.

A nod of understanding spread throughout the group as they prepped themselves ready to enter the dining room.

Pandora led the way, shots instantly firing their way as they entered. As a bullet sped towards Miles, Pandora grabbed his jacket, yanking him backwards and pulling them both down as the group spread out, returning bullet for bullet. Even with the numbers Frankie and Miles had, Joey's boys outnumbered them.

But Joey's boys had no loyalty. Pandora watched as one tried to flee, Joey had also noticed and shot the boy, who couldn't have been older than nineteen, in the leg. He would bleed out slowly but there was nothing they could do at the moment. The boy had obviously made bad choices joining Joey but it was never that simple. Dom had been proof of that.

But Joey couldn't shoot them all and several darted, using what brain cells they had to make a break for it.

Pandora could hear Frankie's voice barking orders from the other side of the room. Someone had been shot, she was getting them pulled out. The blood trailed across the floor as two masked men dragged the groaning body. She recognised the interlinking dragon tattoo on the arm; it was Dom. Her heart sank and her stomach churned as they pulled him out. He was losing too much blood. Her eyes followed as he dragged from the room.

'Time to make you scream, Firecracker,' Joey's voice hissed in her ear as he wrapped an arm around her neck, cutting her air supply as his other hand trained his gun on her head.

'PUT YOUR FUCKING GUNS DOWN OR I'LL PUT A BULLET THROUGH HER!' Joey roared, grabbing the attention of everyone in the room, everyone except the poor boy still bleeding from his leg, desperately gripping his thigh to try and stop the pain and the blood.

They put their guns down, now with Joey's remaining dogs pointing theirs at them.

'Sid, pull her mask off,' Joey ordered the bulky ginger next to him. He yanked it off, her hair springing free as Joey tightened his grip.

'So, this is all you…' Joey growled accusingly.

'I'd like to take credit, but I was just as surprised as you and decided to join in the fun,' Pandora gasped between short breaths.

'If you wanted fun, you only had to ask. I told you, I'd gladly make you scream my dear,' Joey taunted.

'That would require you to be enough of a man to satisfy a woman, Joey. I'm not that good an actress I'm afraid,' she spat with venom, starting to lose vision as his grip held firm.

'Well, we can put that to the test soon enough, after we deal with these rats first,' Joey chuckled.

Joey scanned the room. 'Take your masks off, I wanna see the pieces of shit that thought they could take me.'

One by one they took their masks off.

'What the fuck. A bunch of bitches and you… Miles… you fucking little shit. You'd wish I had just taken your tongue for what I'm going to do to you,' he spat, not releasing his grip.

'Sid, take a few and hunt down any lurking out there,' Joey ordered.

'You sure you don't want us to stay Boss…' Sid suggested.

'You think I can't handle a few rodents?' Joey glared.

Sid knew better than to argue and took four men with him.

'So, who shall we start with,' Joey joked. 'Who wants to go fast and who wants to go slow?'

Joey licked his lips as his eyes fell on Pixie, 'I think I'll definitely go slow with you.' The glare from Pixie made him laugh harder. Joey removed the gun from Pandora's head as her legs began to give out, he aimed towards Jay.

A bullet echoed across the room.

A loud grunt escaped Joey's mouth as he released Pandora, dropping her like a sack of spuds. So focussed on the enemy, he hadn't seen the young boy he'd shot take aim and shoot him in the side of the leg. Payback was a bitch.

'FUCK!' Joey screamed his gun still gripped, he turned to return the favour, but Pixie had already dipped to scoop up her gun, lodging another bullet in his shoulder and forcing him to drop his gun.

Miles, Frankie and the others exchanged bullets with the remaining few men Joey had kept. Lenny crumpled from a shot to the shoulder, the shooter dropping seconds later after a bullet from Lila who had appeared in the doorway.

Lila raced over to Pandora, helping her to her feet, and the pair towered over the scowling Joey. Now reunited with both of his toys.

'He likes to play with his toys so much, maybe it's our turn to play with him?' Lila teased.

Pandora's grin darkened as she dropped to her knees straddling Joey, his arms pinned beneath her. Placing her right hand out, she wrapped her fingers round the handle of the short, jagged knife Lila passed her.

Licking the blade, Pandora looked devilishly at Joey, running her hands through his sleek hair, she grabbed a handful as he grimaced from the bullet wounds. Taking the knife in her right hand she placed the edge across the left side of his neck, his eyes widening as she leant down with all her weight. Her eyes were bright with excitement as she slowly dragged the blade from left to right. Joey struggled desperately as Pandora severed through his jugular, grinning while his warm blood sprayed over her, licking her lips as the last remaining life escaped his body followed by the lifeless look as his head slumped to one side, eyes still wide open.

Lila helped Pandora to her feet, taking the knife out of her hand. She spat on Joey's lifeless corpse, but not before driving her knife through its left eye with a furious scream.

'He's dead Lila,' Pandora sighed, 'he can't feel it you know.'

'Yeah, but it made me feel better,' Lila shrugged putting her foot on his chest and yanking the knife back before wiping it on her jeans and tucking it back into her belt.

Pandora's attention was brought to the slumped over figure; the kid was still breathing.

'Jay, chuck me your belt,' Pandora called. 'Don't get excited, you can keep your pants on, Romeo.'

He chuckled, passing her the belt as she crouched down to the boy who was waiting expectantly for a bullet or a knife. Instead, she wrapped the belt around the top of his leg tightening it.

'Jay, get him some help. Nobody touches him except to help. Understand?' Pandora barked. Jay glanced at Miles who nodded and hooked the kid's arm around his shoulder, beckoning Sparky to grab the other side.

'Looks like it's your lucky day kid,' Jay said as they led him out.

'The house,' Pandora paused, looking at Miles, 'burn it to the ground.'

Miles nodded, as Pandora shakily walked out of the dining room, refusing Lila's help. She would walk out of hell on her own two legs.

Just as she had before.

Forty-Six

Limbo was like a hospital full of walking wounded. Pandora's girls were rushing around under Felix's direction, helping the minor injuries while Felix dealt with what he could. No hospitals. They couldn't risk unwanted attention, especially of the bullet variety.

'Where's Mia?' Pandora demanded as they entered.

'Upstairs,' Storm shouted across the bar, 'Nora is looking after her, she's playing with Izzy.'

Pandora's shoulders relaxed; she'd go check on her shortly but first she needed to check on the wounded. Finding Felix, she looked for an update as he stitched up Lenny's shoulder.

'Stop moving,' Felix moaned.

'It fucking hurts Doc!' complained Lenny.

'Girls get shot and I stitch them up without a sound. Men get shot and moan non-stop!' Felix rolled his eyes.

'How many?' Pandora asked.

'Two dead, one critical and too many to count injured in one way or another,' Felix sighed. He'd never been this busy in one go and his aging face was showing its tiredness.

'Thank you, Felix,' Pandora squeezed his shoulder gently, spotting a body on one of the booth tables.

The bigger club tables had been doubled up as beds and as she approached her heart leapt to see he was still breathing.

'Hey, you,' she said softly, holding his hand, her thumb softly circling his skin.

'Hey,' Dom replied quietly smiling. 'Have you seen Mia yet?' he asked.

'No but she's fine, she's playing with Nora and Izzy,' Pandora reassured him.

'I don't want her to see me like this,' he pleaded.

She nodded, glancing down. His muscular abdomen wrapped in dressings as he grimaced each time he breathed, sleep taking him once more.

'Storm, keep an eye on him please,' Pandora said calling her over.

'Yes, Boss.'

Pixie appeared, covered in blood. Pandora scanned her up and down checking her for injuries.

'Not mine Boss, but you should look at yourself first,' Pixie grinned cheekily.

Glancing in a nearby mirror, Pandora saw the dried flaky blood that decorated her skin. His blood. She smiled darkly, part of her wanted to wear it like a trophy but she didn't want to scare the little ones.

'I'm going to quickly grab a shower, I suggest you do too Pixie,' said Pandora looking her over.

'You never know Boss, some guys might find this look quite hot,' Pixie joked.

Pandora glared. 'Okay, I'm going,' Pixie said, hands up and laughing.

Dipping past the room where the kids were giggling, Pandora headed to the office. Slipping into the bathroom, she shed the blood-stained clothes onto the cold floor. She stepped into the shower, the cascading stream of scalding hot water racing down her skin, dancing with the blood and running down the curves of her body. The burn of the water peeled back the dirty feeling of Joey and his touch, the pain of the heat freeing her from the twisted pain in her heart.

Drying off, her curls dripped down her shoulders as she donned a loose-fitting shirt, high rise light jeans and flat ankle boots. She knocked on the door next to her office, entering slowly so as not to startle anyone.

Three huge grins greeted her, as a small pair of arms wrapped round her.

'Mommy!' Mia squealed, 'Look Mommy, I have friends.' She jumped up and down, pointing at Nora and Izzy who looked equally as pleased.

'I'm so happy Mia,' Pandora gushed, scooping the child into her arms as she rambled about all the fun things they'd been doing.

'Do you know where Uncle Dom is Mommy? He said he'd be back soon,' Mia asked innocently.

'Uncle Dom is a little bit poorly, so he's having a rest,' Pandora explained.

'I'll make him a card to make him feel better!' she bounced, 'Izzy and Nora can help me.'

'I'm sure we have lots in my art box to do that,' suggested Nora. Pandora smiled gratefully.

'Right, you get on with that important job, Mia, and I'll be back in a bit,' Pandora ruffled her hair and put her down to run back to Nora, who was pulling out glitter and paints for the girls. They'd definitely all need a shower afterwards. She'd need to get someone to move her blood-stained clothes from the bathroom first.

As Pandora returned to the office, Miles, Frankie and Pixie were waiting, all looking exhausted.

'So, what do we know?' Pandora asked.

'The last scraps of Joey's boys are running scared,' said Pixie grinning. 'Wayne and Sparky are out with a few of the boys, tying up any loose ends that haven't got the brains to run and hide.'

'What about the boy?'

'Felix has done what he can, he is critical but the next 24 hours should decide,' Frankie explained.

Pandora hoped he would pull through. Second chances were hard to come by but if she could give him one, she would.

'Mr Wyatt, what's your plan?' she asked raising her eyebrow.

'Well, it would seem my sister is more loyal to you than her own flesh and blood,' he grumbled, 'she's refusing to leave.'

Pandora looked at Frankie, who gave her that *I'll tell you later* look.

'My injured can't be moved yet,' he continued, 'so if it's okay with you I'll keep some of the boys you know here to give you a hand and keep an eye.'

Pandora nodded. She was still unresolved on her feelings concerning Miles Wyatt, but she didn't want him dead. That was a start.

There was strength in numbers, especially those that were loyal and if Ciara was loyal to her it meant Miles's loyalty by default. His sister was his world, that was clear.

For now, they all needed each other.

Forty-Seven

Limbo was closed for *'refurbishments'* over the next week as they managed to move the wounded out, one by one.

Nora brought Izzy over to play with Mia most days and as soon as Dom was able to move a bit, Pandora reunited them, much to the pair's delight; they were pretty much inseparable.

Dom entered the office as Pandora watched the girls play on the camera.

'Pan, we need to talk…'

'I already know what you're going to say,' she sighed, waving a hand for him to sit.

'What am I going to say then?' he mused with a smile as he sat on the sofa. He flinched, his stomach still tender.

'That we need to do the DNA test in case she has a family out there,' she trailed off.

They both knew that if she had a family once, Joey would have eliminated them. But she deserved to know the truth. Maybe not today, but one day.

'When you going to do it?' he asked softly, knowing how painful this was for her.

'I already did,' Pandora said, pulling an envelope from the desk, 'I just haven't had the guts to open it.'

'Either way, we both love that kid Pan,' Dom chuckled. 'Never thought I'd hear myself say that, but she managed to get under my skin and I'd move heaven and earth for her. So would you. That's all that really matters.'

Pandora knew the information on that paper wouldn't change how she felt about the bouncy little redhead. But if she wasn't hers and there was a family out there, would she be brave enough to give her back, or would the selfish coward in her win out? What would Mia think in years to come?

Her hands shaking, she tried to open the envelope. She could slit a man's throat but a piece of paper was too much, especially when it held the answer she wasn't sure she wanted to know. She was going soft.

'Open it please,' she begged, sliding it across the desk.

'You sure?' he asked. Pandora nodded silently, downing the golden liquid in her glass, savouring the burn as it glided down her throat.

Reaching over the table to take it, he ripped it open, his eyes slowly scanning the paper.

'Could you read it any fucking slower?' Pandora snapped. Dom's head shot up, one hand rubbing his chin as the other held the letter slowly.

'She's yours Pan,' his voice tapered off.

The sob trapped in her throat as she struggled to breathe.

'The bastard,' she cried angrily, 'all those years... If I could bring him back and kill him again...'

She had mourned, her heart had broken. The pain he had caused had led her to this very moment, to the woman she had become. Dom pulled himself up with a wince, walking to where she was seated. Taking her hands, he pulled her into a soft embrace; she pulled back as his eyes locked with hers. Something snapped in both of them, something long bubbling, left unsaid and never resolved.

The pain flowed freely, behind her office doors she let her tears flow as he held her, his hand softly stroking her back.

Her hands reached up to his face, cupping his large jaw in her petite palms.

Two steps back, her back met solid brick, his arms now caging her between him and the wall. She looked up at him as he towered over her, hungrily devouring her with his eyes, she bit her lower lip.

'Don't do that,' he grumbled.

'What?' she said, biting her lip obliviously.

Dom ran his rough finger across her bottom lip, 'That,' he whispered, 'or I'll have to bite it for you Red...'

He hadn't called her that in years. As it rolled off his tongue, the room got hotter. She clenched her thighs together but she definitely wasn't as dry as the Sahara this time.

'What if I want you to… bite it I mean?' She smiled coyly.

Releasing his arms, he turned his back and a wave of embarrassment flooded her as he walked away.

She heard the click of the lock and Dom turned back with a devious smirk.

'I hope this room is soundproof Red, I'm not sure you want them to hear what comes next,' he threatened in a low growl that made her toes curl and her thighs clench even tighter. Her legs threatened to betray her.

'Why, what will they hear?' she teased as he prowled closer, ready to pounce on his prey.

'You… screaming my name, Red.' It wasn't a threat; it was a promise.

'Many men have said that, yet I'm still waiting…' she said lazily, trying not to show him how much her skin was tingling.

Fury burnt in his eyes. 'Well, none of them will have a chance to try again and I guarantee mine will be the only one you're screaming. You may be the boss out there, but here is a different story.'

His lips descended on hers, devouring her with a hunger that had been building for years. The fire that was building in the pit of her stomach took over as she fought him for control, pulling him closer.

His hands effortlessly popped her jeans button open as he pulled them down to her thighs. Digging his thumbs into her hips possessively, he wrapped a hand around each leg, lifting her on the desk as she fumbled with his belt and button, releasing him.

Pandora took his hand, guiding it to where she wanted it and with his other hand he clenched a handful of fiery red curls, exposing her neck as he continued to nip and feast on her exposed flesh, feeling himself hardening more and more at every whimper and gasp that escaped her lips

The hand she guided slipped lower, reaching its destination. Pulling his hand back he slowly inserted his two wet fingers into his mouth, sucking them dry with a smirk.

'Red, you taste good enough to eat…' he growled, releasing her from her wet lacy red pants, reaching inside her again he teased her, earning another gasp. This time he withdrew, trailing his fingers up to her parted mouth, inserting his dripping fingers as she licked.

'See I told you…' he teased as he pulled his fingers back from her mouth. Her head dipped back as she licked her lips, the need clear in her eyes as she laced her fingers over his boxers, stretched to the maximum, threatening to pop. Looping her fingers into the rim of his boxers she teased them down slowly, freeing him from their constraint.

'God…' she moaned, as his fingers explored inside her once more, the pressure building as he teased and quickened his movements.

'That's not my name, Red,' he growled.

'Dom…' escaped from her lips as her breath quickened and her hips thrust, matching his hands move for move, building until her body clenched up trapping his fingers as she gushed over him.

All control was lost as he heard her moan his name and hooked his hands under her thighs, yanking her toward him on the desk. In one flawless move he thrust into her as deep as he could, gritting his teeth to maintain control as she clenched around him.

'Fuck!' She gasped.

'That's what I'm trying to do,' he smirked, slamming into her once more. Each time she tried to open her mouth to make a wisecrack, he'd thrust into her again, ignoring the pain building in his abdomen. The need to hear her scream his name as he slid in and out of her overtook all other needs as he quickened his pace; edged on as her moans got louder and louder.

'Dom… I'm…' Pandora panted.

'Just hold on, a little more, that's a good girl,' he purred.

Those words sent her over the edge as he slammed into her with everything he had. Her hands by her sides, she gripped the rim of the desk. Pandora screamed, her body clenching against him as she tightened, he felt the throbbing wave bringing him to release just after hers.

As they both came down from the high, Dom kissed her forehead gently sending a blissful shudder down her body as she lay on the desk refusing to move. Dom popped into the bathroom behind the office grabbing two towels. Cleaning himself up he moved onto cleaning Pandora up, helping her off the desk and back onto her feet as she buttoned her jeans back up quietly.

'Dom...' Pandora started.

'What?' he grinned.

'You're bleeding!'

Dom looked down at his soaked shirt. The pain now hitting him like a truck. His knees buckled. All he heard was Pandora's voice screaming.

Well, that's the way to go, he grinned as he slipped into the darkness.

Forty-Eight

'Am I dead?'

'Not yet, but that can be arranged.'

Dom looked at the scolding glare Pandora was firing at him.

'How long was I out?' he groaned.

'Long enough.'

'Fancy round two?' he teased, as her face grew red, and she punched him in the leg.

'Ouch,' he groaned feeling the vibration of the punch, he heard a giggle. They had company.

'Pixie,' Pandora warned, 'pack it in.'

'Yes, Boss, leaving, Boss, right away, Boss,' Pixie chirped, trying to contain her laughter.

'You're a fucking idiot, Dom, you could have bled out!' Pandora snapped once Pixie was out of earshot.

'But what a way to go!' he joked.

'Oh yeah and how do I explain that to Mia, oh sorry, Uncle Dom died trying to get his end away,' she glared.

'I think I was doing more than trying,' he grinned. 'Look I'm sorry I didn't realise till afterwards, I was a bit distracted. You were a bit distracting. But feel free to nurse me better,' he winked, earning him another scowl. 'Look Pan, relax. You've been on high alert for years. Joey's gone. Live a little,' he reached out taking her hand, rubbing circles into the back of her palm. Her scowl softened.

He was right. This was the freest she'd been in years.

'We need to talk Dom.'

'Go on...' he said warily.

'Well, we need to talk about Mia. Limbo will reopen soon and she can't live here permanently. Then there's Izzy, I can't expect

162

Nora to look after her forever, she's a child herself. Then there's you and Mia. And finally, we need to talk about Joey.'

He frowned, 'He's dead.'

'Yes. Exactly. He's dead and he only has one living relative as far as I'm aware.'

'Fuck,' Dom's voice trailed off. He hadn't thought about that.

'Now we know she's definitely mine and his,' the disgust rolled off her tongue, 'she is heir to everything. We've just put a target on a four-year-olds back...' she sighed, the weight of the situation settling in.

'We'll tell everyone she's mine,' Dom suggested.

'Won't work...'

'Why?' he asked, most of Joey's lot were dead. The only people that really knew about Mia were dead or here.

'Well, while you were out snoozing, we received this...' She handed him a letter.

Joey was just the pawn; next move is yours.
The child will be ours.

'What the fuck does that mean?' snarled Dom, crumpling the paper.

'It means Joey was a little fish. Which means all his assets and empire belong to someone else and they want Mia to ensure we don't get them.'

'But we don't want Joey's assets...'

'They aren't going to believe that, they'll want to take her anyway. She's valuable to them.'

'But she's a child, Pan...' Dom reasoned.

'Which makes her even more valuable to them,' Pandora sighed.

'What's the plan then, Red?'

'We play chess of course, and we play to win, my big bad wolf...'

163

RJ MITCHELL

THE BLOOD ACRE

A DS THOROUGHGOOD THRILLER